Charles Stephenson

The Cuban Martyrs and Other Poems

Charles Stephenson

The Cuban Martyrs and Other Poems

ISBN/EAN: 9783337380113

Printed in Europe, USA, Canada, Australia, Japan

Cover: Foto ©Andreas Hilbeck / pixelio.de

More available books at **www.hansebooks.com**

The Cuban Martyrs

AND OTHER POEMS.

BY

CHARLES STEPHENSON.

"Another yet! ye gods I'll hear no more."
" 'The artless Helicon I boast is youth."

ROCK ISLAND, ILL.
THE UNION PRINTING COMPANY.
1874.

TO

ℭaptain Mayne Reid,

WHOSE GENIUS IS EQUALLED ONLY BY HIS NOBILITY OF CHAR-
ACTER, AND WHOSE WORKS FIRST TEMPTED ME
INTO THE PATHS OF LITERATURE,

 **THIS WORK IS DEDICATED**

AS AN

HUMBLE OFFERING OF GRATITUDE AND ESTEEM.

TO THE CRITICS.

DO you look to the Canada thistle
    To find the perfume of the rose?
Do you look to a tin penny whistle
    For the music an opera knows?
For the lilly that grows in the valley,
    Do you look on the mountain-top high?
Do you look for a Byron or Shelley,
    In such a beginner as I?

ERRATA.

Although this department is generally superfluous, I cannot in justice to myself allow the many mistakes produced by careless proof-reading, to go uncorrected. The last word but one of the preface should be "their" instead of "the."

On page 10, line 12, for "angles" read "angels."

On page 41, line 1, for "shrine" read "shrines."

On page 29, line 1, for "gates" read "courts."

On page 147, line 16, for "thin" read "dim."

On page 153, line 4, for "is" read "in."

On page 159, line 5, for "pang" read "face."

On page 151, line 5, for "thee" read "these "

On page 170, line 6, for "Ahey" read "They."

On page 182, line 12, for "earth" read "world."

There are many other mistakes of minor importance, as "boosm" for bosom, "omnious" for ominous, and the substitution of "e" for a. The are two words missing:—"said," in line 11, page 42, and "desert," in line 3, page 189. On page 13, line 8 should read—

"As though the dead could hear the birds."

CONTENTS.

———

THE CUBAN MARTYRS.

Rebellion! foul, dishonoring word,
　　Whose wrongful blight so oft hath stained
The holiest cause that tongue or sword
　　Of mortal ever lost or gained.
How many a spirit, born to bless,
　　Hath sunk beneath that withering name,
Which but a day's, an hour's success,
　　Had wafted to eternal fame!
　　　　　　　　—[LALLA ROOKH.

I.

COME, Freedom from thy mountain height;
　　Come, Mercy, from thy couch of tears;
Come, Justice, from thy throne of Right;
Come all that's good, come all that's bright,
　　Come all that earth to heaven endears,
Come, leave your starry thrones awhile,
　　And wing your flight o'er yonder main,
To fair Cipango's palmy isle,
Where heaven's brightest sunbeams smile,—
　　And smile, alas! in vain;

Where Nature, like a poet's dream,
   Her rainbow banner hath unfurled,
And blushing earth, and glowing skies
Unite to form the paradise—
   The Eden of this western world.
Come, see where all that heaven can give,
   Or nature's hand bestow,
Have been poured out with lavish hand,
O'er hill and dale, till all the land
   Seems like a heaven below !
A heaven in which mankind might be
More blest than angles if but free,
   Nor slavery's fetters know !
Come now, together let us trace
   Each landscape blooming fair,
And learn however Bright the place,
With every charm and every grace,
In vain may nature strive to bless.

   If man be sovereign there !

II.

O'er Santiago's gloomy pile,
   The lamp of heaven is shining high,
And not one mist his brightness dims,

And not one vapory cloudlet skims
    Athwart the azure sky;
Fair as he shone when man was born,
    And earth to being sprung,
(Ere sin had taught mankind to mourn,
Or earth from heaven's embrace had torn,)
    And all was fair and young;
So shines he on this gala day,
O'er Santiago's town and bay,
And earth repays his glances well,
    And with his brightness vies;
Brightly the billows heave and swell
    In measured fall and rise,
While glows each blooming vale and hill
    With autumn's changing dyes.
Within the city's shining walls
    Now youth and pleasure meet,
And many a lightsome footstep falls
    Along each crowded street;
And every heart is filled with joy,
    And every face is bright;
And every breast is bounding high,
And brighter seems each sparkling eye,
    With unlooked-for delight!
Sure must the heavenly choirs be glad

To see such scenes below ;
Sure must perdition's hosts be sad
    That earth such scenes may know :
Sure not the slightest taint of death
    Pollutes these sparkling bowers,
Sure not a sting can lurk beneath
    Such pleasure teeming hours.

III.

O, mockery of God's love to man !
    O, sneer at truth and right !
Sure must the fiends of hell rejoice
    To gaze on such a sight !
Within that city, sheening fair
    As Eden's vernal bowers,
Those streets, by youth and pleasure trod,
Shall run knee-deep with patriot blood
    Ere sunset's glowing hours.
Said I that every face was glad?   .
    That every heart was light?
No! in that city there are some,
Now pent within a dungeon's gloom,
Shall meet a traitor's direful doom
    Ere evening's tints grow bright.

Low crouched upon the dungeon floor,
    In dire suspense they wait,
While through the silence, dread, profound,
Each anxious heart-throb's solemn sound
    Comes like the tick of Fate,
While softly through the loop-hole grate
    They hear the city's hum,
As when the dead can hear the birds
    That warble o'er their tomb,
Then fly their thoughts on Fancy's wing
    To childhood's happier hours,
Those scenes 'round which our memories cling
Through all the changes fate can bring
    'Round these dark lives of ours;
They think of loved ones left behind
    On fair Columbia's shore,
They think of parents long revered,
Of some by tenderer ties endeared,
    They now shall see no more,
For ere the sun shall sink to rest
Behind the hill sides of the West
    Their anguish shall be o'er,
And their enfranchised souls shall be,
In yonder bright eternity,
Blest with, at last, the liberty
    They sought in vain before.

IV.

And why must fall that patriot crew,—
The young, the fair, the brave, the true,
Souls formed by God to dare and do,
    With warm hearts beating high!
Souls formed by God to bless the race,
Souls that a royal court might grace—
    Ah! wherefore must they die?
Why? Go ask Him who made man free,
    Free as the ocean wave,
Who ne'er designed that man should be
    A subject nor a slave;
Go ask that Mighty Power why He
A quenchless love for liberty
    To helpless mortals gave!
Go ask him why within our breasts
    He placed those high desires,
Which ne'er to slavery's foul behests
    Can yield till life expires,
But though like water blood may run,
Still must those lofty hopes burn on
    Like ancient funeral pyres;
Go ask him why the hope was given
To make of earth an earthly heaven,

And then 'twas writ in Fate's decree
That all our worshipped liberty
Should be compelled to bend the knee
    To Slavery's brutal rod,
Until the scourge of tyranny
    Seems like the hand of God !
Those men, condemned so soon to die,
    In manhood's active prime,
A quenchless love for liberty
    Hath been their only crime ;
They dared to wish mankind was free,
As God intended man should be,
    For this they dared to die.
On Freedom's altar laid they all,
With her to stand, with her to fall,
    For her to — all but fly !
To rend the fetters from the slave,
Their hopes, their swords, their lives they gave,
    And gave without a sigh !

V.

Why must they fall ? — Go read what e'er
    Is writ of Spanish rage,

Look backward through the files of time,
Through every age and every clime,
And gaze on every hellish crime
    That stains fair History's page ;
Go read the misery-teeming tales
Of Holland's blood-becrimsoned vales,
    'Neath Alva's tyrant rod !
Go gaze on every blighted scene
Whereever Spanish power hath been
    Or Spanish feet have trod ;
Go read of *Auto* fires that kindle
    In Christ's all holy name,
By whose pale glare even hell would dwindle
    Into a taper's flame ;
Go read of all that hate invents
To torture helpless innocence
    With more than hellish pains ;
Go read of Inca's plundered halls,
And Moctezuma's ravished walls,
    And Hayti's forged chains ;
Go read of many a scene like these,
Until your curdling life-drops freeze,
Then ask why must the page of fame
    Such direful deeds relate !

And groaning History will exclaim
In tones of horror, fear and shame,
    "To glut a Spaniard's hate."
Then come to Cuba's Isle once more,
And see her valleys stream with gore,
Since on her then all spotless shore
    Proud Castile's flag unfurled;
And Spanish feet her valleys trod,
And bowed her chiefs to Spain's vile rod,
And in the holy name of God,
Streams red and deep, of guiltless blood,
    First stained this virgin world!
See her proud chiefs enslaved, enchained;
See her fair land with murder stained;
Then ask why must those heroes die
    For their loved island's liberty!
Go learn from all the shuddering tales
    That History's tomes relate,
That guiltless blood alone can quench
    A Spanish tyrant's hate!

VI.

But hark! That bell! The hour has come,
Brave heroes, of your awful doom!
    Now may ye bear it well.
Loud grates the slowly turning key—

3

Think not it brings you liberty,
    'Tis but your dying knell.
Slow file they forth by ten and ten,
With haughty step and lordly mien,
Sure never nobler souls were seen
    In Sparta's iron land.
Sure not thy pass, Thermopylæ,
Beheld more courage, true and high,
Than shines in every dauntless eye
    Of that devoted band.
Slow file they down the crowded street,
While jeers and taunts and hootings greet,
    To yonder open square;
That square designed of old to be,
A place where mirth and revelry
    Might bless the young and fair.
But now, with glittering uniform,
    And bayonets gleaming bright,
A file of Spanish soldiers stand
Along the square on either hand,
    With looks of low delight.
That low delight that jackals feel,
    When they have in their power
Some noble game that lions kill
    But cannot all devour.
Slow up beside the iron wall

By tens the prisoners file,
For there it is they're doomed to fall,
For their loved native Isle.
With fettered limb and bandaged eye
They wait the word of death ;
But the curled lip, and aspect high,
Betray the true nobility
That still glows bright beneath.

VII.

Hark ! "Fire!" a deafening crash; a pall
Of purple smoke around !
And quick beneath yon iron wall,
Ten lifeless, gory beings fall
Along the crimsoned ground.
"So ! nobly aimed. Another ten,
Brave soldiers. Nobly done."
Another crash—another thud—
Another gush of human blood—
Another ten is gone.
"Another ten; another yet,
And are there still some more ?"
"Yes, twelve remain to meet their fate,
Before the wotk is o'er."
"Well, bring them on. Now once again
Perform your task, my gallant men.

And are there now no more ?"
No.   Of that hapless number, all
' Beneath yon iron prison wall
  Lie weltering in their gore.*
Of all those noble hopes and powers,
  For some high purpose given,
The mangled breast, and marbled brow,
And glassing eye, are all that now
  Remain this side of Heaven.
No; 'tis not all; they leave a name
Which through the brightest page of Fame
  For countless years shall shine;
That noble, but ill-fated host,
Hath formed a gallant holocaust
  To place on Glory's shrine ;
And long as Justice men revere,
And long as Freedom still is dear,
Or ill-starred courage claims a tear,
  Their memory still must live;
And o'er the Cuban martyrs' name,
Shall shine the brightest crown of fame
  That Glory e'er can give.

*The first report of the Virginius massacre stated that 110 per-
sons were butchered; afterwards the number was reduced to 52,
and later to a still smaller number. The poem was written just
after the second report was received.

IX.

Deep as the darkest pall of night,
    Let's draw the curtain o'er ;
Freedom and Justice, Truth and Right,
    Fly to your shrines once more ;
Such smiles as yours should ne'er alight
    On fair Cipango's shore.
Go, fly o'er Russia's snow-clad plains,
And break the peasant's iron chains,
    And bid the serf be free.
Then westward wing your flight awhile,
And bless fair Erin's luckless Isle—
    The Emerald of the sea.
Then to the snow-topped Pyrennees
    Extend your bright domain,
And wave your snowy wings from thence
Above the vine-clad hills of France,
    And olive-blooming Spain.
But o'er the brightest spot that Heaven
Hath to this darkened planet given,
    Your smiles must ne'er be seen.
Freedom and Justice, Truth and Right,
Not for a moment may alight
    On Antilles' blooming Queen;

There Freedom must be quenched in blood;
    There mercy is unknown;
And Right and Justice ne'er have stood
    Around a Spanish throne.
Go, Mercy, and in silence weep;
    Go, Freedom, fold your wings;
Go, Justice, hide thyself in sleep,
In vain ye all your vigils keep,
While 'round the jewels of the deep,
    One galling fetter clings.
Go, and in silence wait the hour,
    When brighter scenes shall be,
For surely if Almighty Power
    Controls our destiny,
The glorious hour must come at last,
When slavery's might shall all be past,
When every fetter shall be cast,—
    And every slave be free.

ROSITA

A Heart Experience.

Yes, the dream at last is over; I can see my folly now;
  See the folly that could blind me into loving such as
    thou!

For I loved thee, loved thee truly; loved thee, but alas,
    too well,
With a depth and with a fullness more than ever tongue
    can tell.

Loved thee more than hot-brained poet ever yet hath said
    or sung;
Loved thee, as my very being upon that affection hung.

Could I help but love thee, when to worship beauty I was
    born,
And to me thou seemed more lovely than the eastern skies
    at morn.

Fairer than all earth's fair daughters; lovelier than a flower
    or star;
Brighter than the dreams of fancy; purer than auroras
    are,

And above my darkened being shone thy beauty beaming
    bright,

As up through the starless heavens shine the rays of north-
ern light.

And besides, my heart was foolish, and knew not the ways
of love,
And I gazed on forms of beauty as on envoys from above;
As on beings sent from Heaven, that humanity might
see—
Might obtain a passing vision of what Heaven itself must
be.

I believed any form that carried beauty's heavenly
impress,
Must be, perforce, a being Heaven-ordained to light and
bless.

O ! the cruel, cruel lesson taught me by a broken heart,
That not always outward beauty has an inward counter-
part.

'Neath the rose's scented blossoms lurks the ever-sharp-
ened thorne ;
From the wine cup's rosy sparkle are the keenest sorrows
born ;
In the sturdiest bosoms often dwells a spirit vile and base,
And a heart more hard than granite lights the coquette's
chiseled face.

Did I deem thee fit for Heaven ? Phrenzied fancy? what
would you,

In a place where outward beauty clothes none but the good
and true?

Thou wouldst be a stranger to them ; they would shrink
from thine embrace

As the life-plant when touched rudely, trembles to its very
base.

Did I deem thee fit for Heaven! Mockery of hope and
faith?

To believe the fields of life could grow the poison flowers
of death.

But my heart was young and foolish, and knew not that
graceful forms

Might be given but as warning of the dearth of inward
charms,

As in some dark street at midnight a low watch-fire meets
our eyes,

Warning us of some deep pitfall that concealed behind it
lies.

O ! my heart indeed was foolish, for as yet my years were
green,

And I worshipped outward beauty, but looked not behind
the screen.

As a child looks at some planet twinkling in its airy place ;
But sees not the dark abyss that yawns beyond in endless
space.

So I gazed upon thy features, saw that they were fair and
bright,
But saw not the heart behind them, blacker than the noon
of night.

I was young, and I was foolish, with impulses running
high,
And my soul went out to worship whatsoever pleased the
eye;

And when beauty shone before me more than e'er I'd seen
before,
What could I but bow before thee, bow before thee and
adore ?

Low, too low, I knelt before thee, till thou motioned me
to rise,
With a smile upon thy lips, and with affection in thine
eyes.

O! that blessed, blessed morning! how it shines through
memory now,
As up through some gloomy valley shines a mountain's
sunlit brow.

O! that cursed, cursed morning! from the moments
wasted there,
Comes a present of keen anguish, comes a future of dispair.

O ! the hour when first I saw thee ; it was long and long
    ago ;
When the trees were void of verdure, and the earth was
    robed in snow,

And the sun withheld his glances, and the north winds
    chilling breath
Swept around till earth seemed slumbering in the winding
    sheet of death.

O, the cold, the dreary winter ! How it pierces like a
    knife,
Emblem of a woman's feelings, symbol of a loveless life,

Then thy beauty shone before me, and the winter passed
    away,
And the cold and bleak December was as warm and bright
    as May ;

And when low I knelt before thee, and thou motioned me
    to rise,
Earth was filled with rainbow beauty, gleams of glory filled
    the skies.

Then thou placed thy slender fingers, placed them fondly
    within mine,
And thou whispered softly, sweetly, "Hubert, darling, I
    am thine !

"All I am, and all I shall be, unto thee my heart hath
given;
I am thine, and thine forever, thine for earth, and thine
for heaven."

As the Æolian harp breathes music when the breezes touch
its strings;
As the humming-bird moves ever in the music of its wings,

So within me and around me music seemed to swell and
float,
Purer than the breath of angels, sweeter than the bulbul's
note.

If all sounds vibrate forever upward through the starry
skies,
Sure those accents charmed the angels in their bowers in
Paradise;

And I said, "My darling, darling, speak those words but
once again,
Surely cherub's harp ne'er trembled to one-half so sweet
a strain."

And thou said them o'er and over, and thou sealed them
with a kiss,
And our souls were joined together in a fellowship of
bliss.

O ! how cold the joys of angels in their pearly gates
    above,
To him whose soul has reveled in the primal kiss of love.

Through my soul that kiss went laughing, leaping like a
    vein of fire,
Till each fibre of my being seemed a lightning-smitten
    wire.

O, that kiss! upon my forehead I can feel it burning
    now,
Burning like the brand of justice on the early murderer's
    brow.

Sign of shame, and sign of sorrow, I can feel it burning
    there,
Telling of the brightest hopes, and of the gloomiest des-
    pair.

Every feeling we experience, be it vile or be it pure,
Leaves a scar upon our beings which forever must endure

If we love, our souls forever seem to bathe in holy light ;
If we hate, our lives are tinctured with the blackness of
    the night.

If these feelings change or perish, the remembrance still
    remains,

Thrilling us with keenest pleasure, piercing us with deepest pains.

Even now that touch of passion through my being throbs
and thrills,
As a lover's lute will echo down the windings of the
hills.

Swiftly flew the moments o'er us, singing us the sweetest
tune,
And the days were always morning, and the year was always June.

O, my God, that we had perished ere those hours of bliss
were past,
Ere the noontide of our passion was with coldness overcast.

O, if there is One all-powerful, watching over us from
above,
One whose very soul is mercy, One whose very name is
love,

Why does He lead us upward to the mountain tops of bliss,
But to blast our hopes, and cast us into misery like this?

Sure for us it had been better if that soul-alluring
dream

Had been quenched in all its brightness in the depths of
    Lethe's stream;

For the dreary hours that followed—O, how dark they've
    been to me,
And but made so much the darker by the memory of
    thee.

Days and weeks flew swiftly o'er us, and the world kept
    on its range;
But we lived within each other, and knew not of time or
    change.

Flew four seasons lightly o'er us, swift as birds of passage
    move,
And our spirits seemed to revel in an atmosphere of love.

Then there came the silent whisper, "Art thou sure thy
    loved one's true?
Art thou sure that her affection centres only upon you?"

O, how firmly can suspicion fasten on the brightest
    name;
O, how quick the breath of slander blights the fairest flow-
    ers of fame.

Like a poison shaft that whisper rankled in my heart and
    mind,

And it put to me the question, "Art thou really then so
    blind?

"Thou art loving a deceiver, one whose only care for thee
Is of thy most cherished feelings to make sport and
    mockery.

Go to her and put the question: 'Darling, wilt thou be
    my wife?
"For the good, or for the evil, wilt thou go with me through
    life?'

"She will smile upon thy folly, talk to thee as to a child;
Tell thee that thy love for beauty must have sent thy fan-
    cies wild,"

As a cloud which in the morning scarcely dots the face of
    Heaven,
Glooms into a driving tempest which shall ravish earth ere
    even,

So that doubt increased within me, crushing out all hope
    and faith,
Driving me to know the truth, e'en though the truth
    should be my death.

The experience of the ages teaches us a truth like this:
That "'tis folly to be wise, so long as ignorance is bliss."

Ignorance induces faith, and faith, methinks, is heaven's
 key;
Wisdom only comes from doubting, and to doubt is misery.

Till that hour I had been happy, earth to music had
 seemed set,
Now the brightest scenes around me seemed o'erhung
 with robes of jet.

Still that whisper hovered o'er me, haunted still my couch
 of rest,
Asking, "Believest thou what I tell thee!" saying, "Put
 her to the test."

Then I went to thee, Rosita, knelt, and placed my hands
 in thine,
Asking thee if still thou loved me, still wert willing to be
 mine?

And thou answered, "As a friend of all thy doings I ap-
 prove,
But I really could not wed me with a soul I do not love.

"True, I thought that once I loved thee, but I then was
 but a child,
And my heart was inexperienced, and my fancy wandered
 wild,

"But the months have brought me wisdom,age has cooled
the fires of youth,
Teaching me that young conceptions oft are very far from
truth.

"I will be your friend, your sister, do not ask me to be
more,
Try forget this foolish passion, seek some other to adore."

O! my God! can this be death? The earth and heavens both are gone!
In the midst of outer darkness stand I, sightless and
alone.

Seems a rushing all around me, seems a humming in my
ear,
Nature revels in confusion, primal chaos sure is here!

No! a light bursts in upon me, breaking slowly through
the gloom,
As the day-light bursts on earth when rising from its
mighty tomb.

Now I see things more distinctly; now I feel the morning
air;
Now I wake to all around me, even to my own despair.

But the sun shines not so brightly, and the skies have lost
    their sheen,
And the birds sing not so sweetly, and the grass is not so
    green.

Earth to me has lost its beauty; it is but a dreary
    waste
Overfull of mirage pleasure, which can ne'er be ours to
    taste.

Once I sought and worshipped Beauty — thought it was of
    heavenly birth,
Now at last my eyes are opened, I can see its little worth.

Clasp a rose to thine embrace, and 't will repay thee with
    a thorn,
Worship at the shrine of Beauty, and 'twill laugh thy
    prayer to scorn.

For I worshipped thee, Rosita, laid my heart upon thy
    shrine,
And thou played with it, as kittens frolic with a ball of
    twine.

Clasping it, and fondling with it for a passing moment's
    joy,

Then in some dark corner cast it as it were a worthless
　　toy.

But stern Truth's relentless finger shall upon thy forehead
　　yet
Write, in signs more black than Cain's was, thy true title
　　of "Coquette."

From that sign who shall redeem thee?　Who shall wipe
　　that curse from thee?
Who shall hide thee from thy memory? from remorse
　　shall set thee free?

Through the busy world thou goest, dost thou find there
　　peace or rest?
Does no dark remembrance haunt thee? do not sorrows
　　fill thy breast?

Aye! though in the crowded city, or upon the lonely
　　heath,
A grim spectre aye shall haunt thee, haunt thee like the
　　hand of death!

It shall haunt thy waking moments, it shall hover o'er thy
　　sleep.
It shall wail when thou rejoiceth, it shall laugh when thou
　　dost weep.

Like th' unswerving hand of justice it shall hover over
    thee,
Forcing thee to share the anguish thou inflictedst upon me.

O this anguish! even now I feel it springing in my heart
And no years shall cool its fierceness, and no balm may
    soothe its smart.

Whither shall I flee to 'scape it? floweth there a stream so
    deep
That the memory may beneath it fall into a Lethean
    sleep?

Shall I snap life's thread asunder? sink at once to death's
    domain,
Where sensations all are over, ceases pleasure, ceases
    pain?

No! for deep within my bosom doth a secret impulse
    lie
Telling me there's that within me which shall never, never
    die.

For the hidden springs of being are not made of mortal
    clay,
They are part of the Eternal, and with him must live for
    aye!

And 'tis this, this deathless portion that most deeply feels
    the wound.
And would feel it though my body were a league beneath
    the ground.

Where then shall I seek for solace? in the cares and toils
    of life?

In the soul-absorbing conflict? in the the "rapture of the
    strife?"

Ere the hopes of youth were quenched beneath the dark-
    ening floods of fate,
I once nourished an ambition, an ambition to be great.

From that fiercest of all passions I some solace may
    derive,
It is still engermed within me, I will force it to revive.

I will plunge into life's battles, I will build myself a
    name,
When I die to leave behind me shining from the cliffs of
    Fame.

I will kneel before ambition, on her altar I will cast
Every moral — mental,— treasure, I will serve her to the
    last.

On the pages of Earth's glory I will carve myself a
name,
Orators shall sound my praises, poets long shall sing my
fame.

Coming ages long shall wonder, long shall wonder and
revere,
And the proudest of the future shall regard me as their
peer.   .

In the cares and toils of labor I will drown the gloomy
past.
All its brightness, all its blackness shall in Lethean shade
be cast.

Let the world roll down its pathway, but let each succeeding sun,
Bring no dark remembrance with it of the winters that
are gone.

Let the waves of fate wash o'er me as upon some barren
shore,
Till my sands of time are ended, till my voyage of life is
o'er.

Then, as sunset's purple glory sinks into the boundless
west

Let my dust be laid forever on its coffined couch of rest.

In some lonely forest valley, on some island in the sea,
Where my rest shall be unbroken by one memory of
thee!

TO A CHRISTIAN;

WHO CROSSED THE STREET TO AVOID MEETING A DRUNKARD.

KNOW ye that that being degraded,
 Containeth a jewel unpriced,
Which though now its lustre hath faded,
 Was bought with the life-blood of Christ?
Know ye that the portals of Heaven
 Were sprinkled with Jesus's blood,
That might be redeemed and forgiven,
 Such wrecks of the image of God?

THE BRIDE OF THE MATTABESSAT.*

A STORY OF UNREQUITED LOVE.

" But Constancy lives in realms above,
   And age is folly, and youth is vain,
And to be wroth with one we love
   Doth work like madness in the brain."
                              — *Colridge.*

PROLOGUE.

IT oft has been said that the shrine of the muses,
   To tropical regions belong;
And that he but the poet's high calling abuses,
   Who seeks for a subject for song
In the cold dreary North,— in the land of the thistle
   Where through ice-covered channels the rivulets flow;
Where in freedom unbounded the hollow winds whistle
   O'er prairies, long wrapt in a mantle of snow.
'Tis said we're scarce colder in clime, than in blood;

---

*This poem was written at fourteen. It is inserted more to "fill up," and
to satisfy those friends who at that time deemed me something of a prodigy, than
for any merit I can see in it now. It was intended to be mock-heroic, but—" alas
that good intentions!" etc.

That of heartfelt affection we know but the name,
While the love of the Southron is "like to the flood
    That surges in Ætna's dark bosom of flame."
But I'll clear thee, my North, from the black accusation,
    Our maidens are matchless, in face and in form,
And the maids never lived in the realms of creation,
    With spirits more tender, or affections more warm,
Though the sun is not robed in his tropical splendor,
    When shining on us of this shivering clime.
Yet our youths are as brave, and our virgins as tender
    And fair as the fairest recorded in rhyme!

    I sing the fate of a Northern maid;
        (The tale for true was told to me,)
    Which proves what I above have,
        As, if you'll listen, you will see.

I.

    "Twas in the month of soft September,
        It matters not what day or year,—
    In truth, the date I don't remember;
        The drooping boughs were growing sere,
    The roses had begun to fade,
        Though still their fragrance filled the air,
    The ripened fruit was hanging red
        In blushing bunches, full and fair.

The birds from in their leafy bowers
    Were sending music through the trees;
The odors of a thousand flowers
    Rode, as in triumph on the breeze.
The rising sun his hues of gold
In waves o'er all creation rolled,
Till every hill, and tree, and spire,
Was bathed in floods of living fire;
The earth was clad in gorgeous sheen,
And all combining, formed a scene
So fair, so peacefully serene,
It seemed an eastern bower of Bliss:—
'Twas on a morn, 'mid scenes like this
    That, as o'er hill and dale I strayed,
I came upon a lakelet fair,
    Upon whose banks there sat a maid
With rounded form and curling hair.
    Her eyes were like a pair of sloes;
Her lips of ruby seemed to be;
    Her cheeks were like the blooming rose;
Her brow of pearl-like purity;
    Her features — face — O! how essay
To tell the beauties of that face,
    When words are powerless to portray
Its more than perfect loveliness;
    I can but say, there's naught on earth,

(And I have roamed it far and wide,
        From east to west, from south to north,)
But what would pale if by her side,
It were but idle to compare
With earthly things a face so fair,
        But think of those bright Georgian maids,
As fair as if from heaven above,
        Who wander through Circassia's glades,
And seemed to be ordained for love ;
        Then think of Spain's dark glancing lasses,
With beauty so supremely blest,
        Whose loveliness, 'tis said surpasses
Of all earth's women kind, the rest ;
        Then think of her whom you adore,
And believe the fairest 'neath the sun,
        Think o'er all these, and many more,
And melt their beauty into one,
        And you a slight idea will gain
Of her who on that morning shone
Beside the lake, but words are vain
To make her loveliness more plain.
Imagination,—it alone
Can paint it, for there ne'er was known
Such beauty elsewhere on this zone !

II.

I said she was such, but in sooth
It would be nearer to the truth
To say that such, it seemed to me,
Was what her beauty used to be,
For now her features seemed to wear,
The wild expression of despair,
And grief, too strong for her to bear,
Gleamed forth in every look and air,
With anger which she ill could hide,
And baffled love, and wounded pride,
Her features were so deeply dyed,
It seemed as though the soul within
Was but a wreck of what had been,
One of the noblest of its race;
And yet, though phrenzy stained her face,
And on her features I could trace
The tracks of hatred and revenge,
And though her look was wild and strange,
And stern her air, yet seemed her eye
As tender as the moonlit sky,
And did a peaceful contrast bear,
To her wild look, and startled air:
Thus war and peace, and bliss and woe,
Did o'er her face their colors throw,

And deeply did those features stain,
With every shade of joy and pain;
It was a face and form, that when
Once seen by mortal, must remain,
In vivid hues for e'er impressed
On the beholder's troubled breast,
And haunt for aye, his couch of rest.

III.

She sat upon a rocky ledge
Which, rising from the water's edge,
In craggy pride the beech o'erhung,
And o'er the lake its shadow flung,
When first beheld, she seemed to be
Rapt deep in mournful reverie.
Her hands were folded, and her eyes
Uplifted to the azure skies,
As if they vainly sought to see,
The secrets of Infinity.
And 'twere an easy task to trace
The different thoughts which seemed to chase
Each other through her troubled brain;
Now wore her face a look of pain,
Anon it passed and in its place
Came one of shame, or deep disgrace,

Until at last, a settled air
Of firm resolve of deep despair,
Was fixed, as if forever there ;
And from her bosom 'scaped a sigh,
And tears stood in her sad dark eye.
She rose, and cast a mournful glance
Across the lakelet's smooth expanse.
Then in a sweet and pensive voice
    She sang of one — a Christian brother,
Who was the loved one of her choice,
    But now had left her for another.
'Twas thus she sang, — I well remember.
    The air was sweet, though stern the words,
And the balmy air of soft September,
    Thrilled with the magic in the chords.

IV.

"Of Arthur, my loved one, I" sure be the bride,
    Though to win him, my life I do spend,
And when by his vows to my apron he's tied
    His parents before me shall bend.
For I cannot give up the one whom I love,
    Nor satisfied be with another,
So through all opposition my way I'll pursue,
    And win him in spite of his mother !

V.

"And should I not win him a life I must lead,
　　Of sorrow, and suffering, and tears,
For my love is at present towards him so intense,
　　He forever before me appears.
And I'd rather lie in a suicide's grave,
　　Than lose him, or marry another,
And I will of a surety self-murder commit,
　　Or have him in spite of his mother!"

VI.

Slowly the words rolled o'er the lake,
　　And up the distant mountain side,
Where lordly trees and tangled brake
　　O'ershadowed far the dancing tide,
And boldly back the echoes cast,
　　In word for word, and tone for tone,
But each more feeble, till the last
　　Seemed like a dying spirit's groan.

VII.

While the maid sang, her look was wild,
　　And filled with stern determination;
That eye, a moment since so mild,
　　Now danced with savage animation.

Her form had undergone a change,
    More fearful seemed her look and air,
As if Love, Hatred and Revenge
    Had doubled all their forces there.
But as the echoes died away,
    And all was silent, save the breeze
Which softly murmured, as at play
    Among the blossoms of the trees,
Methought I saw a pearl-drop shine
    Upon her soft and silken lashes,
Which sparkled like the starry mine
    That from the vault of heaven flashes,
And soon two sparkling streamlets ran
    Like bubbling fountains, from her eyes,
Like those which o'er the fall of man
    Were shed by angels in the skies.

VIII.

While weeping thus a song was borne
    Upon the stilly morning air,
Which startled her, as the hunter's horn
    Startles the wild deer from its lair.
From whence it came I could not tell,
    It seemed to come from every where,
O'er rocky height, through woodland dell,
Across the lake, and through the air,

The breezes seemed the words to bear.
Though loud and clear, I could not trace
Its source to any certain place.
It seemed as though a spirit band,
Had ranged themselves on either hand
And, captivated by the song
  The hapless maid had just been singing,
Were echoing it in fairy tongue,
For on all sides the echoes rung,—
  And in my ear they still are ringing.
In magic measure, through the glades
It softly flowed, and like the maid's,
In word and air was cold and scorning,
  Yet sad and sorrowful in tone,
And echoed on the air of morning,
  Like a dying sceptic's laughing-groan.

IX.

"O! no, my dear Laura, I'm older than you,
  And I'll give you a piece of advice ;
That which you're proposing, you never can do,
  So from trying refrain, and be wise.
My heart or my hand you will never possess,
  So content yourself soon with another,
For I'd rather be hung than be married to one
  Who would have me in spite of my mother!"

X.

These cold words caused the maid to start,
　　A deadly hue o'erspread her face,
Her hands convulsive clutched her heart
　　As though they'd tear it from its place.
It soon passed o'er, and cold despair
Again controlled her look and air.
With folded hands, and flashing eyes,
And look uplifted to the skies,
And bloodless lips, and heaving breast,
She waited anxious for the rest.

XI.

"You say you will surely self-murder commit,
　　If your efforts should prove to be vain;
Why surely, dear Laura, you're crazy or mad,
　　Or else you have 'love on the brain!'
O! cure yourself quick, of this fearful complaint,
　　By catching some fool or another,
And don't think so much of the beautiful one
　　You would marry in spite of his mother!"

XII.

The singing ceased, and then arose
　　A mocking laugh, so cold and sneering,
The laugher must be one of those

Nor man, nor fiend, nor heaven, fearing,
One who once knew his sins forgiven
    But from that lofty summit fell;
Had felt on earth the joys of heaven,
    But 'changed them for the pangs of hell!

XIII.

As fell this laugh on the maiden's ear,
    From 'twixt her lips escaped a cry,
As I hope ne'er again to hear
    In my short journey 'neath the sky:
Then, with wild phrenzy in her eye,
    She rushed towards the water's edge
And wildly waved her hands on high,
    And plunged head-foremost from the ledge.
A splash was heard,—she slowly sank
    Beneath the waters cold and chill,
The wavelets rippled to the bank,
    And all again was clear and still.

XIV.

I reached the bank, and gazed upon
    The tragic scene for eight long hours,
And marked not that the setting sun
    Was sinking to his western bowers,
Till, when the dews were falling fast,
    Benumbed and chill, I rose to go,

Yet one long, lingering glance I cast
Upon the placid lake below,
Then turned to leave, but as I turned,
A ripple on the lakelet's breast
Caught my attention,— I returned
To see what now disturbed its rest.

XV.

I stood upon the jutting steep
From whence the maiden took her leap,
And saw the ripples larger grow,
As if the genii of the deep
Among their coral caves below
The fountains of the lake were troubling,
For like a spring its face was bubbling
O'er where the maiden sank from view.
Fiercer it boiled, and larger grew
The circles o'er the lakelet trending,
Towards the shore their journey wending,
Till their swelling force was shattered
As it met the sloping strand,
And their sparkling drops were scattered,
Like bright jewels o'er the sand.

XVI.

Not long it thus had bubbled, ere,
While watching close, I saw appear
Above the spot which, as I said
Appeared to be the fountain's head,
An infant's form, which seemed to be,—
    So fair, so tender, and so pure,—
    The hapless maid in miniature,—
From sin and earthly taint so free
It seemed, methought my straining eyes
Beheld a cherub from the skies.
But as the moon that moment rose
    Above the tree-tops on the hill,
I saw a sight that nearly froze
    My blood, and made my heart stand still,
For on each side the infant's breast,
    As on the gentle waves reclining,
As though by Satan's hand impressed,
    A hideous serpent's coil was shining.
And through their eyes SIN seemed to stare,
    Repulsive, as all such things are
    Which seem created but to mar
All on the earth that's pure and fair.
Which are regarded — since in Eden
    Through Serpent's wiles our parents fell

By touching of the fruit forbidden,—
    As symbols of the Lord of Hell!

XVII.

Some minutes passed, and then was heard
    A plaintive cry for help, and soon
The maiden's spirit form appeared,
    And claimed the infant as her own.
And now the shades of evening threw
    Their mantle o'er the lakelet's face,
Forever hiding from my view
    The hapless maid's last resting place!

XVIII.

*   *   *   *   *   *   *   *

You'll think that bitter tears I wept,
    But no! there was no cause for any,
The lake wherein the maiden leapt
    Was but the lake of matrimony.

XIX.

The infant that reclined at ease
    Upon the lakelet's mirrored face,
Was what e'er comes of marriages
    Throughout all time, in every case.

XX.

The serpent (hideous thing!) that gleamed
    On either side the infant's breast,—
I ne'er knew what that meant, but deemed
    'Twas *Satan's trademark* there impressed.

"BEWARE OF THE STAINLESS."

WHEN camp-meeting time begins,
        And men grow weary of their sins,
And hang around the Throne of Grace,
With holy looks and lengthy face,
Some pious prayer or hymn repeating —
Then, my boy, look out for cheating!!

A PICTURE FROM LIFE.

The Pope's Vatican at Rome cost fifty million dollars, and holds among its ingredients the sweat, blood and bones of hundreds of millions of ignorant and degraded human beings; and Europe and America are thickly studded over with smaller institutions of the same kind. Like "Alps on Alps" the tall steeples rise, with millions of wealth invested high in air, while under their very shadows Humanity suffers for bread and shelter. All this represents our boasted Christianity and Civilization.—*The Word, Princeton, Mass., Sept.* 1874.

I.

I stood upon a hemlock shaded mountain,
With gleaming landscapes spreading far and wide;
And at my feet a crystal springing fountain,
From a rock's cleft flung out its sparkling tide,
Which rippled lightly down the mountain side
As though it from its source were glad to sever,
And watching as it onward still did glide,
While other streamlets mingled with it ever,
I saw it shine afar, a broad, deep, flowing river.

II.

But ere it reach a river's dignity,
　　And still was but a bright and sparkling stream,
It passed a blooming vale which seemed to me
　　More fair than aught that lights a poet's dream;
　　Where all of Nature's brightest charms did seem
In beauteous harmony to be unfurled,
　　And as the summer morning's rosy beam
Danced on the tide that through it wound and curled,
It seemed a paradise dropped from a brighter world.

III.

For shining there in almost tropic splendor,
　　The brightest hues of ripening Summer shone,
While all that wealth, and taste, and art can lend her,
　　Had added many a charm to Nature's own;
　　And as the sunbeams gayly danced upon
The matchless tints that mingled there and blended.
　　It seemed from Beauty's cornucopia strewn
At random there were all that's bright or splendid
Beneath the mirroring skies which o'er them hung
　　suspended.

IV.

There emerald fields and daisy-whitened meadows
　　Look up to Heaven with ever-smiling faces;

And orchard tufted hills cast lightsome shadows
 On bowers of evergreen around their bases;
 And many a streamlet amorously traces
Its silvery pathway to the parent stream;
 And three small lakelets, from their leafy places,
Peep out to welcome morning's rosy beam,
Pure as an infant's thought, and bright as Fancy's
 dream.

V.

And many a flower-strewn garden there is lying,
 Freighting the breeze with incense sweet and rare;
And spreading fields of ripening harvests, vieing
 With the most lovely scenes that 'round them are;
 And happy flocks in peace are browsing there,
Or lie at ease the green hill-sides along;
 And ever on the odor laden air
Come warbling waves of wild melodious song
From joyous, reckless birds, the shaded bowers among.

VI.

And there are domes of varying shape and size,
 Whose fair white walls attract the passer-by;
Domes of vast structure, and of strange device,
 Wherein the hardy sons of Industry,
 Their time, and skill, and strength unceasing ply;

And temples where is fed the youthful mind ;
    And stores which all the needs of life supply ;
And all that Progress pours upon mankind,
Or Industry can rear, or Enterprise can find.

VII.

And there are cots where humble Comfort dwells,
    In the sweet light of blissful Home's fireside,
Uncursed by Luxury's soul-besickening spells
      Of Indolence, and Ennui, and Pride,
      And all the evils e'er to wealth allied ;
And there are domes no words can e'er portray,
    With noble parks outspreading far and wide,
Wherein the sons of Wealth, from day to day,
In useless indolence can while their lives away.

VIII.

Thus all that Art can give or Nature bring,
    This darkened world to beautify and bless,
Around this lonely spot come clustering
    And make a scene of magic loveliness.
    And were it not that Sin doth still oppress
The face of Nature with her Serpent trail,
    And want, and woe, and sordid selfishness,

Load every breeze with many a groan and wail,
Then might we deem that Heaven were like that
    smiling vale.

IX.

Alas! that even 'mid scenes so bright and fair,
    So full of Nature's sweetest purity,
That even here rebellious man should dare
      To mar her brightness with his infamy;
      And that He who on sainted Calvary
Perished to save man from his primal fall.—
      That His dear name should cloak hypocrisy,
Till Earth grows gloomy as a funeral pall,—
Sure, surely this is the most damning stain of all!

X.

But most 'mong all the beauties shining there,
    Three clustering groups of houses met my eyes,
All standing separate, and different far,
      Each from the rest, in structure and device,
      And there it seemed as life's realities,
Of light and dark at once did gloom and gleam,
      (As darkness on the verge of sunset lies,)
While danced alike the morning's rosy beam,
On Wealth's voluptuous pride, and Poverty's extreme.

XI.

'Tis ever thus since man from Eden hurled
    Lost all the brightness of his first estate,
All o'er the surface of this darkened world,
    Doth Light with Dark, doth Good with Evil mate;
    And where her palaces Wealth would create,
Their shadows fall on Poverty's rude cot
    And where the good, the lovely, or the great
Abound, there most doth evil haunt the spot,—
Such is, and such must e'er be man's unhappy lot !

XII.

O ! that the wisdom of the ancient sages
    Had to the mother of mankind been taught,
So she could look adown the distant ages,
    And view the ruin which her folly wrought,
    Then had the charms the wily tempter brought,
Been brought in vain, and Earth had still been fair,
    As Eden was ere Sin had stained the spot,
And Wisdom's tree, and Life's were blooming there,
And naught was known of want, or sorrow, or dispair.

XIII.

But it was done ! The glory of Creation.—
    The master-piece of the Creator,— fell,
And now Earth's want and woe and degradation,

How deep that fall hath plunged mankind, doth tell,
To every age and clime, alas! too well,
What sowed the Sires, the Sons in sorrow reap.
  The crime of one hath made this earth a hell;
And Sin doth still her dreary burdens heap,
And earth in want and crime for ceaseless ages, steep.

XIV.

And is this justice?   Aye, it must be so!
  For the Eternal One hath it decreed,
That on the children's head shall fall the blow,
  Which was by right alone the parent's meed,
  That guiltless hearts shall for the guilty bleed,
And Sin's black shadow darken Time's abysm,
  And on the Woman's unoffending seed,
With the dread certainty of Fatalism,
Shall shower the withering shafts of 'vengeful Despotism.

XV.

And since the breathing of that fiendish curse,—
  "Cursed be the earth forever for thy sake,"
The mingling forces of God's Universe
  Have striven of earth a slaughter-house to make.
  The pestilence, the avalanche, earthquake,
Volcano, famine, sickness, battle, storm,
  Have sapped men's veins this Demon's thirst to slake,

And man beneath the rod must writhe and squirm
As 'neath his own rude heel doth writhe the helpless
    worm.

XVI.

The elements combine to work our death,
    And tinge our lives with misery's deepest dye.
Each passing breeze is but a poison breath,
    Surcharged with venom from the great Most High,
    Which 'twere but vain to fight, but vain to fly.
Around, behind, before, below, above,

    Where'er beneath the dome of yonder sky
Mankind may chance to be, or live, or rove,
They wither 'neath the scourge of this vile God
    of Love.*

XVII.

There's not one drop of water in yon stream;
    There's not in yonder mount one grain of sand;
There's not one ray of light in summer's beam;
    There's not one fraction of the sea or land
    But helps to forge destruction's iron band

---

*I suppose many persons will call this language downright blasphemy and Atheism, but I cannot help it. The fault is not mine, but belongs to those who invented the God-idea. For if we accept the Biblical hypothesis of Deity, the only logical inference to be deduced therefrom is that He is responsible for the accumulated miseries of all past and present ages, and as much deserves our hatred for the existence of evil, as our love for the existence of good.

And swell the increasing sum of human pain.
    The poison shafts from the Almighty's hand
Fall thick and fast upon us, as the rain
Falls on the earth when thunderclouds are rent in twain.

XVIII.

And so the world stands now: That simple taste
    Of fruit, whence man would wisdom fain derive,
Hath made this earth a dark and dreary waste,
    Where man in ceaseless care and toil must live,
    While want and crime around him strain and strive
(As vultures quarrel o'er some new-found prey)
    To make him all their own, and weld the gyve
Which Sin hath forged ; and win the fight which may,
Man, helpless man alone, the loser is alway.

XIX.

So ran my thoughts, as from that mountain hight,
    Afar o'er many a rapturous scene I gazed,
And marked that in that valley of delight
    Which there in all the hues of summer blazed
    That even there had Superstition raised.
And Wealth cemented, and Religion sealed
    A barrier 'twixt mankind, which Custom glazed,

O'er with a web of seeming right, which veiled
But ill, the pride and crime, which there had fain
　　concealed.*

XX.

I said that as I o'er the valley gazed,
　　Three clustering groups of houses met my eye;
First on a vernal summit proudly raised,
　　Their slender steeples pointing to the sky,
　　Two noble temples stood, where the Most High
Received the homage of his trusting saints,
　　When they around the Altar gather nigh,
To lay thereon their longings and complaints
And plead for cleansing from whate'er the soul
　　attaints.

*Of all the curses which afflict mankind there is none more blighting in its effects than the inequality of social conditions, unless it is the Supernaturalism which first inspired, and has since upheld it. The superiority of one class inevitably produces ignorance and poverty in the inferior classes, and these evils have ever been the most fruitful source of misery and crime. In all ages the struggle between Capital and Labor has produced the most widespread evils, and it will continue to do so until every social barrier is torn down and men shall stand on a plane of perfect equality. The French Revolution, our own civil war and the Paris Commune were some of the fruits of this social upas, and to-day the moral atmosphere is charged with miasmatic currents and omnious clouds are massing in oposite points of the heavens. The black clouds of Labor roll up heavily in one direction while over against them loom the yellow masses of Capital. These opposing forces are slowly emerging towards collision. If they meet, the storm that follows means Revolution and it will be universal and thorough. ,

Doubtless there are many who will think me mistaken in connecting, Religion with this evil, but, waiving all debate as to the origin of the evil

XXI.

And there they stood in spotless white arrayed,
    Objects to love, to worship, or revere,
As the beholder's mind is easiest swayed
    By awe, devotion, reverence, or fear ;
    And Wealth and Fashion weekly gather here,
In formal stateliness, reserved and cold,
    While ordained lips pour in the willing ear,
The truths by universal love unrolled,
To men who weigh mankind in sordid scales of gold.

XXII.

And worshippers in gorgeous silks and satins
    Kneel reverently upon the frescoed floor,
And breathe from heartless lips, inspired matins,
    To Him whom they are gathered to adore ;
    And pour devoutly for the suffering poor

there is no fact more patent than that the Church of Christ is the strongest
support of the CASTE system. In all countries, except the United States,
the priesthood, as a class, are the outspoken opponents of equality and
republicanism, and they would be so here if they dared. But as they
dare not, they talk glibly of equality and at the same time fawn upon and
flatter the rich in order that the latter may surround the church with a
halo of Aristocracy through which the poor man can only penetrate with
reverence and awe The front seats of the synagogues are reserved for the
snobs while the workingman humbly takes the uncushioned seat by the
door, and even there is only tolerated on account of the contribution box.
I venture to say that no poor man would be allowed in any church if it
were not that their combined "mites" lessen the draft on the rich men's
pockets.

Prayers which methinks must choke them as they come,
    For ne'er within that consecrated door
May Poverty, though pure as Christ, find room,
Save he who sweeps and lights, and warms the holy dome

XXIII.

And there they stand, upon that vernal hill,
    O'er looking scenes miraculously fair,
Whence oft the Sabbath's consecrated bell
      Tolls sweetly on the morning's balmy air,
      Th' appointed day and hour of praise and prayer,
And there are many who will meekly hie
      To pay their homage to their Maker there,
Who deem His brightest works which 'round them lie,
It were a heinous crime to covet or enjoy.

XXIV.

O! when shall man from Superstition's trance
    Awake, and learn that all that is, is God?
That Law, and Harmony, and the vast expanse
    Of Nature, spread on every side abroad,
    Are all we need to serve, or can, or should.
When shall we learn that faith; and praise, and prayer
    Are mockeries? That Usefulness and Good
Are synonims? And Happiness, howe'er
Secured, is all for which mankind need seek or care?

XXV.

O! all-sufficient Nature! thou who art
    The uncreated mother of us all,*
The infinite whole of which we are a part,
    Thine only is the shrine at which we fall,
    Thou only art the God on whom we call,
The source of life, and light, and happiness,
    The eternal friend, the only all-in-all,
Not in such man-made temples is thy place,
But in thine own broad fields we meet Thee face to face.

XXVI.

But He who in yon temples is adored
    By the elect and fortune favored few,
Well fitted is he to become the Lord
    Of that devout, and proud, and canting crew,
    Naught with mankind hath such as he to do
Save to destroy and wage an endless war.
    And as the lord, so is the servant too,—
Not made of common clay—the worshiper,
And He who is adored are matched in character.

XXVII.

But turning from these mockeries of mankind,
    Which Earth have long insulted and disgraced,

*"I behold in matter the promise and potency of every form and quality of life."—JOHN TYNDAL.

Another cluster of proud domes we find,
　　Like them, upon a green-clad summit placed,
　　Where wealth and art their beautious homes have traced,
And added many a charm to Nature's fairest,
　　For surely all the soul can wish, or taste
Suggest, of all that's loveliest and rarest
In Nature, or in Art, that vernal hill-top wearest.

XXVIII.

There lavish hands a lordly park have spread,
　　With shading bowers of deathless evergreen,
By Nature's gleaming emerald carpeted;
　　And perfumed beds of ripened flowers between;
　　And sparkling founts are there in crystel sheen;
And pebbly walks in curves fantastical
　　Wind, serpent-like around and through the scene,
And at the base a lakelet, clear and cool,
Shines up in heaven's face, supremely beautiful.

XXIX.

And on the summit of that eminence,
　　Their fair white walls hid by a shady bower,
Two noble domes in proud magnificence,
　　Above this scene of nymphean beauty tower
　　In the proud majesty of conscious power,

And all that endless riches can command,
    Have lavished there a right imperial dower,
And gems of art from many a distant land,
And all that's bright and fair, within those temples
    stand.

XXX

And noble dames, with blood as blue as heaven,
    There dwell in ease, and luxury, and pride,
And Sires whose locks the hand of time hath given,
    That silvery tinge nor wealth nor art may hide,
    And noble youths and maidens there abide, ·
To want and woe and labor all unknown,
    And gilded servants through the hall-ways glide,
As puppets hover 'round a monarch's throne,
Co-sharers with their lords of glory not their own.

XXXI.

And many a laughing party there assembles,
    From all the high and proud for miles around,
And lightly on the air of evening trembles
    The thrilling strains of social music's sound,
    And merry footsteps o'er the carpets bound
In the bright mazes of the circling dance,
    And seem the hours to be with pleasure crowned,

And joy beams forth in every sparkling glance,
And revel reigns supreme till morning's hours advance.

XXXII.

And thus they while their useless lives away.
    'Mong scenes that almost seem like heaven on earth,
Revel by night, and idleness by day,
    And ease, and indolence, and reckless mirth;
    But 'mong the joys to which their wealth gives birth,
There still is missing Nature's brightest gem,
    For true nobility and manly worth,—
Those brightest jewels in earth's diadem—
'Mong all their gilded joys, these are unknown to them.

XXXIII.

'Mid all these scenes which Nature spreads, and Art
    Has beautified, there yet is lacking still,
That nobleness of mind or soul, or heart,
    Which, call it by whatever name ye will,
    Is yet the one thing needful to fulfill
The law which Nature gives us; and which can
    Cause us, 'mid all our want and wealth, to feel
That but one blood flows in the veins of man,
Like far diverging streams that in one fount began.

XXXIV.

But let us leave this scene to view the third :
    Adown the valley as I gaze afar.

There meets my eyes a scene which doth afford
    Strange contrast to those other scenes, which are—
    Or seem—like heaven, so beautiful and rare;
And are those really houses that I see?
    Can those rude huts, so like a wild beast's lair—
Can those dens human habitations be?—
Aye, and far worse than these, 'neath withering poverty!

XXXV.

But let me look again!   Can it be believed
    That those vile dens are human dwelling places?
Yes! they are so; my eyes were not deceived,
    Though would they had been, for, while it amazes,
    A scene like this the gazer's soul debases,
To think that such a state should dare exist
    Where Nature thus hath poured her charms and graces,
Were like that scene in years agone, I wist,
When first in Eden's bowers the Serpent squirmed and
    hissed.

XXXVI.

What is it that I see?   I look again.
    A group of houses down the valley's side,
Though some look far more like a wild beast's den
    Than dwellings wherein mankind should abide;
    Yet some there be which taste has beautified,

With all the arts that Poverty can wield,
    And 'round their gardens with a worthy pride,
Wild flowers, fresh culled from Nature's blooming field,
Are spread, and heavenly light and fragrance freely yield.

XXXVII.

And there the noblemen of Nature dwell,
    The hardy sons of tireless Industry,
In whom no want, or woe, or work, can quell
    The patent-right to true nobility,
    And though around their homes Humility
And Meekness dwell, yet there doth Comfort bless,
    And Beauty cheer, while Taste harmoniously
Twines 'round their cottages in sweet caress,
A maze of perfumed vines, in magic lovliness.

XXXVIII.

And if we step within the humble dwelling,
    Through doors 'round which the morning-glory blooms.
We find a scene of beauty far excelling
    The gilded glory of the gorgeous domes
    Where wealth and art, and plenty have their homes;
For here is peace, and purity and joy—
    That holy joy which e'er from virtue comes,—
And love and friendship their sweet arts employ,
Nor ennui mars their bliss, nor doth repletion cloy.

XXXIX.

And when are gathered evening's purple shades,
    What scenes of joyousness are gathered here!
The wearied sire the dust of toil abrades,
    And 'round the cheerful hearthstone draws him near,
    While prattling children gather 'round to cheer
Him with their merry looks, and smiling faces,
    While she to him almost as heaven dear,
Greets him with cheering words and fond embraces,
And love as pure as that in heaven's holiest places.

XL.

But all are not like these; as we emerge
    From this bright scene, and 'round us cast our eyes.
We see there standing on the outer verge
    Of this bright group, a gloomy hut which vies
    With the most squalid dens beneath the skies;
Naught see we there but wretchedness and want,
    And all the outward signs of sin and vice,
In heaven's face their banners boldly flaunt,
Like some foul fiend of crime, sent this bright Vale to haunt.

XLI.

With straw-thatched roof, pierced by full many a rent,
    Through which the wind and rain find free access,
And from within afford an easy vent

For stench and smoke which there are in excess,
    And low rough wall which windows ne'er did bless,
But only loopholes welcome morning's ray;
    And such an air of squalid wretchedness,
Around the whole, and such a vile array
Of filth and dirt, the soul, besickened. turns away !

XLII.

And if we enter this rude domicile,—
    A task to try your nerves right well, I ween—
We find that inwardly 'tis full as vile,
    As outwardly 'tis wretched and unclean.
    For everything degraded seems, and mean,
And naught but filth and dirt do there abound,
    And Poverty on every hand is seen.
Or where its wolf hath left its bleeding wound,
While Sin her serpent-coil hath twined the scene around.

XLIII.

A tattered blanket serveth for a door,
    Two rough hewn blocks are there, for chairs instead ;
The bare, damp earth affords the only floor ;
    And straw and husks on a dried ox-skin spread,
    May serve alike for sofa, or for bed ;
A rough stone fire-place in one corner is —

By rotten stumps and dead-wood branches fed,
While on one side, on a rude shelf there lies,
A few, and but a few of life's necessities,

XLIV.

And they who dwell there ! who and what are they ?
    Not gilded sons of luxury, I trow !
But those in whom licentious passions sway,
    Has stamped the name of outcast on the brow ;
    Embodiments of all that's mean and low,
The scum of earth, the garbage of creation,
    Who Law, nor Decency, nor Gospel know,
Nor aught but want, and filth and degredation,
Such are they who have made this hut their habitation.

XLV.

A man and woman, if to call them such,
    Be not a libel on the very name —
And in good truth, they look not over much
    Like those who on the hill-top, in a flame,
    Of glory, live, 'mid all that wealth can claim,
But with low brows, and sin-distorted features,
    And faces proof 'gainst modesty and shame,
And all wherewith Vice loves to paint her creatures,
They stand, of sin's effects, the world's most eloquent
        preachers !

XLVI.

And it is little reck they of the law,
    Divine or human, modern or antique,
Nor Custom's bondage doth their spirits awe,
    Nor Superstition's ever-changing freak ;
    To live as best they can is all they seek,
Nor care what others do, or say, or think ;
    To them the Sabbath is like all the week :
And all Religion's rites seem but a link,
Of that dark chain which binds them to Starvation's brink.

XLVII.

And there they live the vilest of the vile,
    In filth, and want, and general wretchedness,
And not one cheering word or friendly smile,
    Illumes the darkness of their deep distress.
    And not one ray of goodness seems to bless
Their dark domain — but is it really so ?
    Is no dim spark there, which might intumesce
If warmed by love ? as from the mines below,
The earth, are brought to light the fairest gems that glow.

XLVIII.

We all have faults, some more, perhaps, than others,
    Or seem to have, but who may judge the heart ?

Or who may say, since all mankind are brothers,
  Who most deserves that sentence dire, "Depart?"
  Perchance they who in yonder domes of Art
Revel in godly luxury and pride,
  May feel more keenly God's avenging dart,
Than these vile beings, when the Crucified,
Shall come again to judge the world for which he died.

XLIX.

Thus in that valley mingle shine and shade,
  The light and dark, the righteous and unholy,
Which ever thus their twinings interbraid,
  Since our first mother's act of maddening folly,
  Which still prevents the light from dazzling wholly,
From every taint of gloom and darkness free,
  Nor yet may gather gleamless darkness solely
Above or 'round us ; such is Fate's decree,
Or God's — no matter which — Amen, so let it be !

HEAVEN.

WHEN the modern Christian dies,
 The last thought flashing from his brain,
Anent his mansion in the skies,
 Is, " *how much gold will it contain?* "

SOLITUDE.

—

WHO hath not longed, when Disappointment's
blight
Hath robed the future with the hues of night,
When sorrow, failure, toil, and pain and care,
Have filled the soul with feelings of despair,
Till, worn and jaded with the ceaseless strife,
It grows o'er weary of the voyage of life,—
Who hath not longed, when these dark moments roll
In floods of blackness on the gloomy soul,—
Who hath not longed for some wild, woodland glen,
Far from the busy scenes and haunts of men,
Some cool, secluded nook, or mossy glade,
In some dark forest's over-hanging shade,
Where, by some fountain's flower be-spangled brink,
The soul can lie at ease, and freely drink
The holy impulses that nature brings
When the soul drinks at her unpoisoned springs,
Where no rude taunts, or sneering jests may greet,

To mar the silence of that lone retreat.

O there is bliss, a bliss as deep as heaven,
To souls by grief and disappointment riven,
To while away the hours in solitude,
In the cool fastness of some lonely wood,
Far from the trials, struggles and defeats,
Which in the world the weary spirit meets,
Upon some mossy pillow to repose,
Heedless alike of treacherous friends and foes,
And free from thoughts of grief, and carking care,
Hold sweet commune with lonely Nature there,
In drowsy indolence to lie reclined,
With spreading branches o'er you intertwined,
While reckless birds the rustling leaves among,
Pour out wild waves of sweet, melodious song,
And all that's bright, and beautiful, and pure,
As nature can be, when from man secure,
Weave their sweet spells around the lonely spot,
Unmarred by one foul wish or evil thought,
With not one trace of human kind, to tell
That aught of nature e'er from nature fell.

O oft, how oft! when heart-sick with the strife,
The ceaseless wrangling of a darkened life,
When disappointment, pain, and toil, and care,

Cast o'er my soul the shadows of despair,
Till, with no star of hope to glad my eye,
My weary soul would fain lie down and die,
How oft I've longed, in such deep wretchedness,
For some sweet place of refuge such as this,
Where I could leave the darkened world behind,
And cool the fever of my raging mind,
And soothe my aching spirit into rest,
With life's elixir, drawn from nature's breast.
I knew of such a spot in childhood's day,
When life was young, and roses strewed the way,
Whence oft I fled, when life's dull burdens pressed
Too heavily upon my boyish breast ;
It was a heavenly spot, a place in which
The voice of nature to the soul might teach
More of the good, the noble, and the true,
Than endless tomes of man-made laws could do.
Deep in the cool recesses of a grove,
Where few of mortal kind e'er deigned to rove,
Far from the busy scenes which mortals tread,
When by the world's engrossing pleasure led,
By the bright margin of a shaded pool,
So deeply pure, so brightly clear and cool,
It seemed more lovely than that crystal lake,
Where angel maids on high their toilets make,
The azure violets that crowned its rim,

Seemed duplicated in its crystal brim,
Till, through its lucid depths the pebbly bed
Seemed with the smiling blossoms carpeted,
While the wide branches of the trees above,
A leafy canopy had interwove,
Through which, through rifts by fluttering leaflets
      made,
The noontide's dancing coruscations played
Upon the surface of the lake, as light
As moonbeams fall upon the face of night.
And as the winds of morning softly played
Among the branches canopied o'er head,
The leaflets, fluttering in the murmuring breeze,
Seemed trembling with Eolian harmonies,
And springing violets, from emerald beds
Of velvet moss, were lifting up their heads,
And deathless myrtles, amorously wound
Their clinging tendrils, the tall trunks around,
And in the topmost branches, far above,
A song-bird poured his matin psalm of love,
And praise to Nature, rich, and sweet, and pure,
As all things are when from man's touch secure.

How oft, when Childhood's ceaseless trials came
Upon my soul, in floods of grief or shame,
And life seemed heavy, have I sought this bower,

To 'scape the gloom of Disappointment's hour.
What'er my woe—remorse, or shame, or grief,
Alike my spirit here found sweet relief,
And dozed away the anguish teeming hours,
On beds of emerald moss and springing flowers,
Dreaming bright dreams, alas! too bright to last,
Of some near future, brighter than the past,
How oft I lay upon that fountain's marge,
And leaving fancy free to roam at large,
Down in its crystal depths, methought, beheld
The glory of the years to come, unveiled:
When crowding thickly on my teeming brain,
Came dreams of glories I was soon to gain;
Dreams where, of all the triumphs yet to be,
I saw the greatest centred all in me.
I saw myself,—or dreamed, or thought I saw,—
The object of earth's reverence and awe,
A favored being, 'round whose brilliant name
Were hung the brightest glory wreaths of fame,
I saw!—but who is there hath never seen
When Youth's imagination lifts the screen
From future years, himself emblazoned there,
In Glory's galaxy, the brightest star?
Such dreams come oft to all in Childhood's day;
They came to me, as listlessly I lay
Upon that fountain's brink, a refugee

From life's dull cares, and boyish agony ;
They came, alás! and quickly fled, and left
My soul of all sustaining hope bereft.
They came and went,—the brightest dreams of youth
Are falsest as they most resemble truth !
And they were false, and never realized,
And yet for weary years how fondly prized !
As backward o'er the past my fancy roams,
No hour of joy upon my memory comes
And thrills so sweetly through my soul, as those
Spent in that glade in indolent repose,
When o'er the years to come my fancy roved,
Dreaming those dreams of future joys, which proved
When by the eager spirit once embraced,
Like Dead Sea fruits, all ashes to the taste,
Yet how they thrilled me then! when life is young,
And hearts beat high, and hope is bright and strong,
Those evenescent visions seem to be
More real and life-like than reality,
But they were false! that future now is past,
And seems with darkest thunder-clouds o'ercast.
Down the long avenue of backward years,
Not one oasis of delight appears,
Save those bright hours, when, by that fount reclined,
I dreamed of glories I was ne'er to find.

Long years, and many a mile, now intervene
Between me, and that blissful hour and scene,
Yet oftimes now, the thoughts which drove me then
To seek the solitude of that sweet glen,
Impel my soul to long for some such spot
Where earth's dull care and turmoil cometh not,
And there, with none to mourn me weeping nigh,
In solitude to lay me down and die.
For what is life, by naught but failure crowned?
Or earth, with naught but deserts scattered 'round?
What is existence, rifled of success?
What future years, when hope hath ceased to bless?
Far better, far, on Nature's welcome breast,
To sink at once, and sink for aye to rest,
Than linger on, till weakness or disease
Shall put an end to life's infirmities,
The hour that comes to all, must come to me—
The hour when all that is must cease to be;
The sooner come, the sooner past and o'er
And disappointment then will haunt no more.
And if I now knew of some lone retreat
Like that which blessed my youth, methinks 'twere
    sweet,
Among its springing flowers again to lie,
With warbling birds, and murmuring fountains nigh,

And there, unseen, sink sweetly to repose
On Nature's bosom, out of which I rose,
Far from the world, far from mankind, with none
But birds and flowers to know my soul had gone.

SAMPSON.

WHEN the Scriptures declare that Sampson the
    bold,
   Stopt ten hundred Philistines' breath,
With no weapon except the jaw-bone of an ass,
   Does it mean that he "jawed" them to death?

DREAMS.

I had a dream, a wild and darksome dream,
  One of those pictures which the imagination
Paints to itself in morning's dreamy silence;
When the deep stream of slumber undisturbed
Flows through a narrower course, and its bright drops,
Laugh o'er the pebbles of a shallower bed ;
When, lightly as a summer cloud doth hang
Trembling, between the earth and azure sky,
The never-resting spirit floats along,
The shadowy boundary of things unseen,
And the rough verge of dark reality,
Touching on both, yet resting upon neither.

How wonderful are dreams ! how strange and wild
Their mystery-teeming workings ! Beautiful,
And bright, and new each time they burst upon
The memory laden mind, and yet how old !

Old as the breath of life !   All things that be,
Or have a being, or have ever been,
Since first in Eden's blossom shaded bowers,
The Sire of all who groan beneath life's burdens,
Felt the life-giving breath of Deity, have dreamed:
And while the Universe shall still revolve
Around itself, and earths, and stars, and suns,
Shall breathe with life, and life shall glow with hope,
And love, and passion, and desire, still all
That live shall dream, and still the dreams shall be,
As bright, and fresh, and new as April mornings.

How wonderful are dreams !   A mystic blending,
Of life and death, of quiet and unrest,
An intertwining of the chains of slumber,
With the wild thoughts and hopes, and memories,
Of busiest scenes of life — the biting anguish
Of disappointed hope, the sting of pain,
The agony of fear, and darker yet,
The gloom of deep despair ; with the wild joy,
Of hardly won success, the bliss of love,
The thrill of pleasure, and the sense of pride,
Are felt as keen, aye ! oft times far more keenly
Than when, in Life's arena bravely fighting,
Their wounds are given and received, and leave

Their scars upon the soul forever! while 'round
Them all—the pleasures and the pains—a sense
Of real unreality, which seems
To softem them, while it intensifies,
Floats softly as a lover's sigh, upon
The dewy breath of even, and hangs o'er
The forms impressed by them on memory's wall,
A dreamy veil through which they scarce appear,
When wakefulness assumes her sway again.

How wonderful are dreams! the mind imprisoned -
When daylight's rosy ocean floods the earth,
By the dark walls of care, and toil, and strife,
And dire necessity, whose iron bands,
Enchain the star-throned intellect within,
The tread-mill of Existence — the intellect
Is freed in dreams. Before their mystic touch,
The barriers of habit are o'erturned, and forth
The enfranchised genius soars on chainless wing!
Then the o'er burdened mind, all faint before,
Now, on fresh pinions, soars to higher summits,
In the domain of Thought; or deeply dives
Into the fountains of Profundity, and brings
From thence her brightest gems; or through the caves
Of Mystery, will wander on and on,

Unraveling each and all of her dark windings ;
Then, o'er Imagination's rosy fields
Light Fancy flutters on enraptured wing,
Flying from sweet to sweet, and flower to flower,
As butterflies float o'er a daisy field,
Dropping their honied kisses everywhere ;
Then Memory's magic wand waves o'er the past,
And all that's dark or bright stands out again,
Upon the walls of Time ! The budding childhood,
The flowering youth, the ripened manhood come
Floating adown the stream in bright confusion,
And springing thence gay Hope leaps farther on,
And spreads the Future's rosy meadows out
Like a rich feast before us, and invites
The impatient soul to cull from thence the brightest,
Of fruits and flowers, and make them all its own,
Strange mingling of the time that was, and is,
And is to be ! Harmonious intermingling
Of Fancy's rosy dreams with the bleak desert,
Of hard reality ! Sweet harmony,
Of Memory's keys, when played upon by Hope.

OSCAR'S BRIDAL.

BRIGHT are the lamps in yonder hall,
  And bright the faces shining there,
And sweet the laughing peals which fall
  Like music on the evening air,
  For laughing spirits young and fair,
With youth's impulsiveness and pride,
  In pleasure's circle mingle there
Uncaring for the world beside.

Bright is the scene that sparkles there,
  And gay the laughter-echoing crowd.
But all without is bleak and bare,
  And night winds whistling shrill and loud,
  And from yon darkly lowering cloud
That hangs is heaven's gloomy hight,
  The feathery snow flakes like a shroud
Envelop earth in spotless white.

Bright is the scene that shines within,
    For 'tis young Oscar's bridal even,
She whom he long essayed to win,
    To him at last her heart hath given,
    And wealth, and art, and taste have striven,
To weave their brightest garlands now,
    And earth awhile seems linked with heaven,
To smile upon their bridal vow.

Bright is the scene! but look outside,—
    Who yonder feebly staggers on ?
Methinks her features glow with pride,
    As fall those sounds her ears upon,
    See, up the steps of marbled stone,
She steps and rings with palsied hands,
    And anxious waits until some one
Within, shall come for her demands.

With silvered locks and wrinkled brow,
    And form o'er-bent with toil and care—
Such is Oscar's mother now,
    Such is she who is waiting there,
    And though her garb be worse for wear,
And by rude winds of winter riven,
    Yet matchless tenderness is there,

And love as pure and deep as heaven.

Hark ! footsteps from within draw near,
　Now widely swings the opening door ;
" Tell Oscar that his mother's here,
　Whom he so loved in days of yore,
　Tell him his mother fain would pour
Her blessing on his fair young bride,
　Go — I will linger at the door
Till Oscar calls me to his side !"

" I know her not !" the youth replied,
　When told his mother longed to bless,
" Think you I can my darling bride
　Upon her bridal eve disgrace ?
　Go bid her seek some other place,
Nor strive to mar my hour of bliss,
　Her crooked form would hardly grace
A scene of pleasure such as this."

O ! there are blows that sometimes fall
　Upon these weary hearts of ours,
More crushing to the soul, than all
　The darkest fate upon us showers.
　'Tis when Ingratitude o'erpowers

The heart that once in love hath rested ;
　O! then should death at once be ours,
For all that makes life dear, is blasted.'

How bears this blow that mother's breast ?
　She gives no wild, despairing shrieks,—
Ah! such had ill the woe expressed
　Beneath whose pang the spirit breaks.
　A moment pausing ere she speaks,
She breathes a wild, but sad reply,
　While tears are coursing down her cheeks,
Like rain-drops down a summer sky.

"I loved you once, I loved you well,
　I nursed you when your life was young,
And through your infancy's sweet spell
　I o'er your helpless cradle hung,
　And soothing lullabies I sung,
When pain would ne'er of rest allow,
　And wound my hands your locks among.
To chase the fever from your brow,—
To be repaid, as I am now.

"Farewell! your bridal I had blessed
　Had I been welcomed to your door,

Now may a mother's curses rest
 Upon your life forevermore !
 O, better had I died before
An hour, a scene like this drew nigh!
 Since Oscar loves me now no more,
Naught, naught is left me, but to die !''

The door is closed, the dance goes on—
 But who in yonder snow-drift lies,
Motionless as the piles of stone
 Which all around in grandeur rise?
 With death's cold glitter in her eyes,
And snow-like palor on her brow,
 Young Oscar's lifeless mother lies,
Killed—murdered—by that fatal blow.

* * * * * * * *

What sound is that in Oscar's room ?
 What means that pistol's echo there ?
Some soul hath surely met its doom,
 Else why that yell of wild despair?
 A lifeless corpse lies bleeding there,
Its hand a pistol clenched around,
 'Mong papers telling how and where,
His murdered mother had been found.

Wild is young Oscar's widow now,
  As, bending o'er his lifeless corse
She marks upon his clay-cold brow,
  His murdered mother's parting curse,
  Full well the stinging of remorse,
Hath paid that act of heartless pride,
  Hath paid it with a self-made corse,
And with a widowed, maniac bride.

ART VERSUS NATURE.

SAY, would you view a work of Art,
  Which doth all Nature's charms excel?
Go walk through any public mart
  And gaze upon a modern Belle!

FELO DE SE.

— -

CALMLY as the march of death,
　　Rolls the crystal tide beneath,
　And invites to slumber there ;
While afar the Church bells' pealing,
Through the evening silence stealing,
　　Seems to call my soul to prayer !

As two currents fierce and fleet
In some narrow channel meet,
　　And in conflict fierce engage,
So the peal of yon sweet bell,
And the river's mystic spell,
　　In my breast a conflict wage.

'Neath the river's swelling breast,
Surely might my spirit rest,

Calmly as an infant's sleep,
Surely earth's dull care would never
Haunt my soul again forever
   In the bosom of the deep.

Floating idly hither, thither,
Reckless where, or whence, or whither,
   Wafted like a wind-tossed plume ;
Memory's brightest scenes before me,
Gurgling music rippling o'er me—
   Where exists a sweeter tomb ?

Sure to him who there reposes,
Sweeter than a couch of roses,
   Must those gurgling waters be !
While each wandering, wavy billow,
Presses like a downy pillow,
   Through a bright eternity.

Shall I try them — help me, Heaven !
Be the impious thought forgiven,
   But — how dark my life has been !
Friendships scorned, and efforts wasted,
Hopes but cherished to be blasted ! —
   Sure the leap were hardly sin !

O'er the meadows of the past,
As my memories backward cast,
  Dark as night the scene appears,
Dreary hours of griefs and sorrows,
Dark to-days, with darker morrows,
  Crowd each other down the years.

Morn and noon of life's brief day,
Passed, nor saw the sun's bright ray—
  Evening now around me closes,
Through them all, stern Fate's decree,
Like a lauwine showered on me,
  All life's thorns without its roses.

As the bud is, so the flower ;
Weakness ne'er engenders power ;
  Ne'er from darkness springeth light ;
What is dark by Fate's decree,
Must while it hath being, be
  Shrouded o'er in deepest night.

So the future, like the past,
Seems with thunder-clouds o'ercast,
  Far as hope may dare to soar ;
Disappointments, sorrow, gloom,

Seem my fate pre-destined doom,
  'Till I reach the other shore.

O ! thou gently swelling billow,
Wherefore should I fear to pillow,
  On thy breast this aching head ?
Are the future's fields so pleasant,
Or so bright the past or present,
  "Twere not better to be dead ?

Years made up of cloudy morns :
Boundless fields of roseless thorns ;
  Are they then so dear to me ?
Are my very pangs so dear,
That to 'scape them I should fear
  To seek Lethe's stream in thee ?

Hopeless, helpless, and despairing.
Earth and hell against me warring.
  Wherefore should I struggle on ?
Every day, and every morrow.
Only adds a deeper sorrow,
  To the ones already gone.

Yet I cannot! 'twere ignoble,
Thus in death to flee from trouble
  Which is but man's lot below
Life is robed in hues of jet,
But the tomb is darker yet —
  Off! thou tempter, let me go!

What! because my heart is weary,
And the road is dark and dreary,
  Basely from it shall I fly!
Never! till my work is done,
Till my allotted course is run,
  'Twere but cowardice to die.

Though my life be robed in sadness,
Such a step were more than madness —
  What dost thou present, fair river,
But long years of nothingness?—
Better far to bear distress
  E'en though it should last forever!

Better far to bear the woes
Fortune daily 'round me throws,
  Until death's appointed time,

Life is dark, but darker far
All such thoughts of madness are,—
  Grief was ne'er so dark as crime !

Still—but no, I will not listen,
Billows, gaily may you glisten,
  Laughing onwards to the sea,
Bright the sunbeams playing o'er thee,
But more dark than the weeds that floor thee,
  Than e'en life has been to me.

Hark ! again that mystic pealing
Like an angel's voice comes stealing,
  Softly through the evening air.
Sweet as mother's voice it seems,
Heard above our infant dreams,
  Poured for us in evening prayer.

Heaven be praised ! that holy token,
Hath Despair's dark bondage broken,
  Hope once more unveils her face,
Light again is shining o'er me,
And an angel's hand before me
  Beckons to the Throne of Grace !

Let me go, nor faint, nor falter,
Till I've knelt me at the Altar
   By Almighty goodness given ;
Let me learn, and let me know,
Earth has ne'er so dark a woe,
   But its balm is found in Heaven !

WOMAN.

"NONE but the brave deserve the fair."
   Is often writ in Fiction's tome,
And we may add that none would dare,
   (Except the brave,) to live with some.

THE REASON WHY.

YOU ask if I'll ever get married,
    And settle down in life?
You tell me 'tis every man's duty
    To take to himself a wife.
I'll admit that perhaps you are right, sir,
    That man cannot flourish alone,
And that every man's life is a failure
    Who earns not a home of his own.

But in this extravagant age, sir,
    Pray, what can a workingman do?
If a man barely lives when he's single,
    Pray, how will he manage with two?
An honest man's bills must be paid, sir,
    If they cannot be paid when alone,
Pray what will he do when there's added
    The bills of a wife to his own?

I'm a working man, sir, and not lazy,
    I work my full hours every day,
I have no unneedful expenses,
    And surely don't squander my pay,
And yet, be I ever so saving,
    Every penny I've laid up would go,
Should I happen to run out of business,
    Or be sick for a fortnight or so.

Suppose I should take me a wife, sir,
    Some angelic sort of a girl,
And the dark-colored spokes should come up-
        wards,
    In the wheel of Fortune's whirl,
I could laugh at misfortune myself, sir,
    But could I ask her to share?
For a man, you know, laughs at misfortune,
    That would ruin a woman to bear.

Then the women! I'm fond, sir, of reading
    Of those of the olden time,
Who with hearts full of love and devotion,
    Have made their lives sublime,
But now, should you search the world over,
    (It grieves me the thing can be said),

You'll find that from this dreary planet,
   Those olden time girls have all fled.

Just walk down our streets some fair day, sir,
   And look at our fashionable girls,
Sailing on like a bundle of ribbons,
   All silks, and satins, and curls,
They are fair to the eye, I'll admit, sir—
   So are all modern triumphs of art,
But devoid of all beauties of nature,
   And poor in the riches of heart.

The poorest young girl of to-day, sir,
   Must dress in silk, satins and gold,
She must blaze with glass stones, and paste jewels,
   Till she dazzles the eye to behold,
To outshine a rival in lustre,
   Is to them quite a heaven below ;
And the frowns or the sneers of Mrs. Grundy,
   Are the only perdition they know.

Suppose I should get one of these, sir,
   Whose life is bound up in her dress,
And who knows of house keeping, as much, sir,

As I of the planets, or less?
Only think how my wages would fly, sir,
    For her fancy, unnec'sary robes,
Till in less than six weeks from the day, sir,
    I'd be poor as a turkey of Job's.

What a workingman wants for a wife, sir,
    Is not a mere bundle of clothes,
Nor a body made up of steel corsets,
    Nor cheeks of the *colour de rose*,
What he wants is a heart that can cheer him,
    A mind to encourage and guide,
And a friend that through trial and trouble,
    Will stand ever close by his side.

The life love of any true woman,
    Is of all earthly pleasure the crown,
And when I can find one of these,
    I'll talk about settling down,
But now I can only, like Moses
    When standing on Canaan's shore,
Gaze afar at those regions of promise
    To which I can never pass o'er.

But just let me hint, sir, in parting,
     If you know where I'd probably find,—
Not a bundle of silks and of satins,
     But a wife of the old fashioned kind,
Just tell me where she resides, sir,
     And the wind shall be slower than I,
Till I've laid all I am at her feet, sir,
     Determined to win her, or die !

JONAH AND THE WHALE.

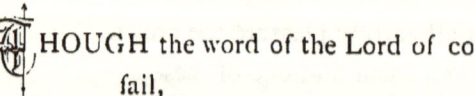 HOUGH the word of the Lord of course cannot
     fail,
     And 'twere blasphemy surely to doubt it
Yet methinks 'twere as easy to swallow a whale,
     As to swallow that story about it.

THE ORANGE RIOT.

———

New York, July 11th and 12th, 1871.

"Yet Freedom, yet thy banner torn, but flying."
Streams like the thunder cloud against the wind."
—*Byron.*

I.

AND has, alas! the fatal hour arrived
   When to a brutal, foul-faced Mob's decree,
The Law, from which our freedom is derived,
And which should guard it, basely bends the knee?
Has this fair land -- the birthright of the free,—
Become the plaything of the slaves who come
O'er ocean's face, from foreign tyranny
Upon our happy shores to find a home!—
Their only refuge place beneath high Heaven's dome!

II.

Ah ! little did our glorious fathers dream
That ere ten short decades should pass away,
The first century of Freedom's dying gleam
Would light such scenes as we have viewed to-day,
Who would have thought a Mob's unholy sway,
Could shatter thus the bulwarks of our land,
And TREASON boldly walk our streets, while they
Who're called the people's champions, trembling stand,
And Law and Justice walk with Murder hand in hand.

III.

Yet such is what we see! the sacred right
Of all who seek beneath our flag a home,
To honor that in which their souls delight,
Must be foregone at the command of some
Foul hearted slaves of power-aspiring Rome,
Oh ! if our hearts can give one manly throb
Should we not blush to see free men become
The crouching slaves of such a brutal mob,
Whose only rules of life are : "Pillage ! burn ! and rob !"

IV.

Aye ! blush Columbia ! for thy holy name
Becomes through this the laughing stock of kings ;
No more needst thou thine " Equal Rights " proclaim,
For they are gone with other, meaner things ;
List to the gibes which Despotism flings !
Mark how they say with many a scornful jeer,
" Freedom, like wealth, oft takes itself to wings,"—
O ! that a freeman should be forced to hear
Such insults to the land his soul should hold most dear.

V.

And is this all of Freedom ? — this the last
Short stage of human Progress ? — must the earth
Go through once more the dread ordeal she passed
A century ago at Freedom's birth ?
Will ever, Liberty, thy proper worth
Be seen by those thou hast so much at heart ?
Will all the sects from east, west, south and north,
In serving thee, e'er take a generous part,
And thou be borne aloft all glorious as thou art ?

VI.   ·

Will thou e'en live through this? yes! o'er the land
A cry of indignation rises clear,
And starting at the people's loud command.
Behold the LAW upon the scene appear,
Armed as in days of yore, with JUSTICE' spear!
And mark how soon she lays the traitors low!
Their foul attempt shall cost the makers dear,—
See how they fall! a wretch with every blow!
And our fair streets and walks with their warm life-blood
       flow!

VII.

But soon the conflict ceases, and high o'er
Her treacherous foes, doth Right assert her reign,
And Freedom's starry banner waves once more,
Nor bears upon her folds one single stain,—
Cleansed from all foulness by that crimson rain,
In terror now the traitors slink away!
Will they the lesson need to learn again?
Will they from this learn wisdom? or will they
Repeat the foul attempt in which they 've failed to-day?

VIII.

Alas we fear so ! the impetuous throng,
Who strove to-day from Freedom's brow to tear
The brightest of her laurels, will not long
In sullen silence their chastisement bear ;
Even now their threat'nings rise upon the air,
Even now, upon the eve of their defeat
We see them for another day prepare ;
While yet their comrades' corpses block the street
We hear them vow once more, with Freedom to compete.

IX.

Not all the blood in Orange Riots shed ;
Not all the shame of eighteen sixty-three ;
Not all the ridicule heaped on his head,
Can make the fire-brained son of Erin, see
That this great land is, must, and shall be free ;
That that for which our fathers fought and died
To make a land of Right and Liberty,
Must ever be the freeman's hope and pride,
Though for it, hireling's blood shall crimson every tide !

X.

Yes ! though that shining sun shall set in gore,
And our fair mountain streams all crimson flow ;
And War's dread tempest sweep from shore to shore,
With its attendant train of Crime and Woe,
Yet still triumphant over every foe
Shall Freedom's starry banner be unfurled,
And still her sons shall to fresh conquests go,
Till tyranny shall from its throne be hurled,
And Liberty's bright beams illumine all the world.

CHRISTIAN TREASURES.

FOR mortals to lay up their treasures in Heaven,
    Is the beautiful precept the Savior hath given,
And his children proceed to acknowledge its worth,
By commencing to *lay them up here on the earth.*

THE JUNE OF LIFE.

O! brightest time of the teeming year ;
    O ! sweetest of all life's hours,
How long will it be ere the dreary waste,
Of a darkened life, will again be graced,
    With thy bright-blooming flowers ?
Never ! the roses of June are spread
    But once in all the year,
And only once will the journey of life
Pass over the meadow that erst were rife
    With the roses we deemed so dear,
A few short months and the charm is gone,
And the dreary gleam of a winter's sun
    Will see them withered and sere !

THE DRUMMER OF GRAVELOTTE.

COLDLY and proudly the queen of night,
 Looks down on the dead and the dying,
Where scattered thick o'er the field of fight,
 The trophies of death are lying,
Thousands of hearts which an hour ago,
 Pulsed high with the hopes that o'er-run them,
Now quiet, and calm, are slumbering low,
 With the hand of Death upon them.

On a swelling mound, where the corpses lie,
 Like shaeves on a wheat field lying,
In a drummer's dress lies a fair-haired boy,
 Shot through the breast, and dying,
A blue-eyed boy, in his teens as yet,
 In the bloom of boyish beauty,

Though his mild blue eye seems now re-lit,
    With the manlier light of Duty.

With his head reclined on his shattered drum,
    He seems like a warrior sleeping,
But the crimson drops from his breast that come,
    Prove that death his watch is keeping,
He is not yet gone for his pulses move,
    Though soft as the sigh of a lover,
And only too soon will he soar above,
    Where the din of war is over.

The raging of battle at last is o'er,
    And his comrades gather near him,
But his lease of life seems renewed once more,
    As afar from the spot they'd bear him;
"O! bury me here, on the spot where I fell,
    'Tis the place for a soldier's grave,
Where the flowers above the winds may tell
    That I died as becomes the brave."

Here he paused and choked, while the clotting
        blood
    In his throat, began to rattle,
" Tell mother I died as a soldier should

Who falls on the field of battle,
Tell her I fell with my face to the foe,
    Who were fast before us flying,
And tell her—and brother—and sister, too,
    That I—thought of them—when dying.

"And bury my drum—with—," a heavy sob,
    And his soul is across the river,
And his youthful heart gave one last throb,
    And its pulsing ceased forever,
And the glassing eye, and the stiffening limb,
    And the more than earthly beauty,
Are all that remained on earth of him,
    Who resigned all else to Duty.

They buried him there with his drum beside,
    And they planted the cold turf o'er him.
And a comrade came at morning tide
    And a heart-felt prayer breathed for him.
And planted a flower on the new-made mound,
    That bloometh from morn till even,
And sheds a mystical fragrance 'round,
    Which seems like the breath of Heaven.

A MEMORY.

'TWAS only once, and years agone,
    In ripening manhood's early prime !
She shone before me like a dream,
An image formed on fancy's stream,
As bright as morn, as soft as even,
As fair as light, as pure as heaven,
She seemed a vision, sent to bless
My being with her loveliness,—
She shone before me!—but since then
Long years of toil, and care and pain,
Have in succession fled away,—
And yet it seems but yesterday !
In memory still her beauties gleam
So bright, the years like moments seem,—
    The thinest web of time.

'Twas but a moment, and 'twas gone ;
    The vision vanished as it came,
As when a pall of darkening clouds
The sunlit vault of heaven enshrouds,
Through some thin rift, a struggling ray
Of summer sunshine finds its way,
To glad the earth awhile, and then
Withdraw behind the clouds again,
So, through the clouds of fear and strife,
That darked the heaven of my life,
Her beauty for an instant shone,
To light and cheer me, and was gone,
Was gone — as visions must depart
Too bright for earth, and left my heart,
    With hopeless love aflame.

Since then, long, weary years have fled,
    Long years of darkness and despair,
And grief and pain, and care and toil
Have sported with my fate the while.
Till the long, bleeding lapse of years,
Seems dim with sighs, and wet with tears,
But I could bear, and not complain,
If she would come but once again,
And with her loveliness, illume

The dreary darkness of my doom,
But she is gone, and gone forever,
As pictures fade from off a river,
Fxcept in oft returning dreams,
In which her loveliness still seems,
    As fair and bright as e'er.

And now my race is nearly run,
    I'm nearing time's extremest shore,
And all around my struggling bark
The waves of fate are drear and dark,
But through the darkness still there gleams
That phantom of my early dreams,
As in a dream she floats before,
And beckons to the farther shore,
And points beyond, and whispers, " Then,
My Darling, we shall meet again!"
Yes, we shall meet, shall meet once more
Where dreams and sighs, and tears are o'er,
And I will wait, and believe that when
Our fates shall intertwine again,
    'Twill be to part no more !

THE DEATH OF CHILDHOOD.

I.

AN evening star eclipsed in blackest night ;
  A morning sun by thunder-clouds o'erhid ;
A summer sered by early autumn's blight ;
A fountain, dammed ere it hath left its bed ;
A budding tree which proudly lifts its head
While cankerous worms its roots of life consume ;
A rose, frost-bit ere it hath time to shed
Upon the breeze its life-bedewed perfume, —
All these are types of Beauty blasted ere its bloom.

II.

To mourn for these in man were surely wise :
The tear of fond regret is wisely given,
When all we love, when all that's lovely, dies, —

When Beauty's blossom from its stalk is riven,
E'en though as we would believe, to bloom in heaven ;
Who can repress an inward shuddering
When darkness shrouds the purpled dome of even,
E'en through to-morrow's sun be sure to bring
Day-beams again as bright as those now taking wing.

III.

And when in childhood's prattling innocence,
The withering hand of death alights upon
Some budding flower, in whose bright liniaments
We deemed the rays of life immortal shone,
When all of purity earth e'er has known,
The brightest flower that e'er on earth appears,
When fell decay alights on such an one,—
When death takes all that loveliness endears,
All that we know of truth, say ! shall we check our tears?

IV.

No ! let us weep, weep heartfelt tears for them ;
The gushing tear, the sigh of fond regret,
Becomes the coldest, when the brightest gem,
That ever gleamed in Beauty's coronet,
Is ta'en from earth, e'en though to be re-set
In brighter worlds on high.   O ! there is still,

A hope for him whose cheeks with sorrow wet
At infancy's decay ; who yet can feel
At childhood's death, his heart with pangs of sorrow thrill.

V.

Aye! let us weep for them, but not forget
This lesson, taught us by their young decay—
Though morning's sun be hid in darkness, yet
A golden sunset crowns the darkest day,
And Bows of Promise smile the clouds away ;
And so, though grief our hearts may break, yet even
Through deepest darkness comes a cheering ray
From this sweet promise, by our Savior given : —
" All such as these are mine, of such as these is Heaven."

A LOVER'S FAREWELL.

FAREWELL ! the hour has come at last
  When our linked fates for aye must sever,
The bonds Affection 'round us cast,
  Are broken now, and broke forever !
And now no more on earth for me,
  May Passion move, or beauty bloom,
My heart is dead to all but Thee,
  And never may its life resume.

As in the heavens, the evening star
  Through twilight's melting darkness gleams,
So thy sweet face, though holier far,
  E'er shone resplendent in my dreams,
And lured me with its holy light
  To fairer fields, and purer skies,
But now that star hath set in night,
  And never more for me may rise.

Then why, since every hope hath fled,
    Should I live longer here below ?
Far better slumber with the dead,
    Than live to bear this weight of woe,
And yet I would not seek relief
    In Lethe's deep, unconscious sea,
For even my bitterest hours of grief,
    Are sweet with memories of Thee.

How oft I've dreamed, in boyish pride,
    Of happy scenes in years to come,
When thou'dst be ever by my side,
    The guardian angel of my home,
Those happy scenes I ne'er shall see,
    Fate hath for us a different doom,
That we shall part, is his decree,
    Till bound in union in the tomb.

And thou wilt be another's bride,
    And naught but joy and peace shall know,
And year on year with thee, the tide
    Of life, shall calm and blissful flow,
Sweet scenes of home shall thee surround,
    Fond friends shall to thy wishes bow,

Till, in the joys that hem thee 'round,
 Thy life shall seem a heaven below.

While I, in scenes of care and toil
 Must try to soothe the ceaseless pain,
The dark despair, the wild turmoil,
 Which rages now through heart and brain,
And while my life and memory last
 Must try forget I e'er could love,
And drown the bright and blissful past
 In the wild scenes through which I rove.

And yet, though we are doomed to part,
 And ne'er may meet on earth again,
Yet still I feel, I believe thy heart
 Is mine, and mine must e'er remain,
And oft, amid the joys of home,
 When light and gay thou seem'st to be,
In sorrow will thy spirit roam
 To him thou never more mayst see.

And as the swallows, when the leaves
 Tell of the coming wintry time,
Forsake their homes beneath the eaves
 To seek a more congenial clime,

So from the cares and toils of life.
   Till it hath passed death's dreary bourne,
From bliss and woe, from peace, and strife,
   My spirit shall to thee return.

Yes! though our lives are doomed to run
   In different pathways, yet I ween,
Our hearts must ever beat as one,
   Though leagues of oceans roll between,
And when shall come the hour that parts
   All earthly things,—and come it must —
That hour for aye shall doom our hearts
   To sleep in undivided dust.

THE SUICIDE.

Nor sought the self-accorded grave,
Of ancient fool or modern knave.
—*Byron*

"FOOL or knave!" I hear you crying!
 O! say not those words again,
Of those weak ones who by flying,
 Would escape life's toil and pain,
Would escape the woes that greet them,
 Every step they onward take,
Till the heart too weak to meet them,
 Must be silenced, or must break.

Life is dark, and life is dreary,
 And the world's a desert waste,
And the heart grows often weary
 As it journeys on in haste,—
Journeys on in haste to meadows

Which are lying just beyond
Where the palms cast cooling shadows,
    And the fountains murmur 'round.

Darkness shrouds the ever-present,
    With a ne'er dispelling gloom,
While the future's iridescent
    With a glory yet to come,—
With a glory coming ever,
    That is ever on the way,
For though bright the morrow, never
    Doth the brightness shine to-day.

O ! how faint the spirit groweth
    Under hope too long postponed,
Longing for the light that gloweth.
    In the region just beyond,
When the mirage, slowly fading,
    In the distance lingers yet,
Mocking with its light, the shading
    Of the present's hues of jet.

Why then wonder if the spirit
    Sometimes falters on the road,

If, too faint. too weak to bear it
   It should sink beneath the load,
Sink, and seek relief from sorrow,
   And life's never rifting gloom,
In the brighter, calmer morrow
   That awaits us in the tomb.

They whose souls have felt the iron
   Of a disappointed hope,
Felt that foes their lives environ,
   With which they can never cope,
They can feel for those whom sadness
   Driveth on to do and to dare,
Do and dare those deeds of madness
   Which but rivet their despair.

Let us view then with compassion
   Those who weary in the strife,
Who in hours of reckless passion
   Snap apart the thread of life,
Think perhaps had we been tempted
   By misfortune's darker powers,
From which faith hath us exempted,
   Then their doom had been but ours.

Let us then, on those whose trials
    Prove more than their souls can bear,
On whom Fate hath poured her vials
    Of misfortune, and despair
Let us look upon them kindly,
    Pitying their awful doom,
Who thus weakly, but not blindly,
    Seek a refuge in the tomb.

SAMSON.

THAT Samson was a man, the Scriptures tell.
    But I'm inclined to think he was a woman,
Because he used to "jaw" so wondrous well,
    Which as we know, with women is quite common.

ONWARD.

—

ONWARD, onward, ever onward !
  To the mountain top aspire,
If you aim your arrows sunward,
  Though they never reach the sky,
They'll be sure to go the higher,
  From their being aimed so high !

Onward, onward, ever onward !
  If you'd gain the laurelled crown,
Backward steps are always downward
  On the up-hill road of life,
And the victory 's only won
  By pressing onward in the strife.

Onward ! 'tis by his own doing,
  Every man is small or great,

Only to assiduous wooing
  Fortune will her smiles impart,
And the only rule of fate
  Is found within a dauntless heart.

Surely in a world like this is
  Where success but waits the winning,
Where the smile of Fortune, blesses
  Only those who onward press,
Sure we are not free from sinning
  If we do not win success !

Onward, onward then, forever !
  Never fainting, never weary,
Never looking back, and never
  Thinking that defeat may come,
Though the road is dark and dreary,
  And the goal is wrapt it gloom.

Onward ! with a faith believing,
  And a purpose firm and true,
Trembling with no dark misgiving
  As you journey day by day,
For there's victory waiting you.
  If you faint not by the way.

DREAMS OF CHILDHOOD.

I AM lonely to-night, and with gloom overcast,
  As musing I sit in my chamber alone,
For my mind wanders back o'er the fields of the past,
  And lives once again in the days that are gone.

I dream of the days of my earliest youth,
  When my spirit, just launched on the ocean of time,
Borne merrily on by the billows of truth,
  Set sail for Eternity's harbor sublime.

The days when existence knew not of a past,
  And the future was glowing with rose-tinted dreams,—
Ah me ! 'tis the future that now is o'ercast,
  While the time of my childhood !—how happy it seems,

In fancy again shine the happiest hours
   That gladdened my soul in the bright long ago ;
In Memory's garden, the loveliest flowers,
   More brightly than ever, seem blossoming now.

Each scene that I cherished again re-appears ;
   Through each childish delight I am living once more ;
But so changed have they been by the fleeting of years,
   That I scarcely would know I had met them before.

How wide seems the gulf 'twixt the past and the present,
   When measured by counting the years as they pass !
How narrow the gulf, and the vision how pleasant,
   When seen through the magic of Memory's glass !

How tedious the moments then seemed, and how slow,
   How thick with the sorrows of childhood o'ercast !
How pleasant, how happy they seem to me now,
   When tinged with the mystical light of the past !

The moments then seemed to be moments of sorrow,
   And life seemed o'erhung with misfortunes and fears ;
Now the one supreme joy which from fancy I borrow,
   Is to dwell on the joys of those earlier years.

Sweet days of my youth, will ye ever return?
  Shall I ever re-visit thy joy-teeming shore?
No, long though the lamp of existence may burn,
  The days of my childhood shall glad me no more.

Never more, never more, shall the pathway of life
  Be illumed by the bright careless pleasures of youth,
Till I've done with Earth's falsehood, and sorrow and strife.
  And rest in Eternity's haven of Truth.

MILLENIUM.

"THE time shall yet be," wrote a prophet of Zion,
    "When the lamb shall lie down side by side with
        the lion."
And the truth of this prophecy no one need doubt,
Since the lamb will be inside, the lion without.

A LAMENT.

WHAT matters it how men may come?
　　What matters it how men may go?
To me, an outcast, doomed to roam,
　　Where'er the tides of Fate may flow,
Or Fortune's breezes choose to blow—
　　A lonely waif on Fortune's sea,
Forever wafted to and fro
　　By the wild waves of Destiny.

What matters it what doom be mine?
　　The same to me are weal and woe,
Though Fortune's smiles upon me shine,
　　Or adverse tempests fiercely blow :
Since not one faithful friend I know,
　　To whom my pangs or joys are known,

But through life's vale of tears I go
    Forever friendless and alone.

What matters it though all be dark,
    That shines for me no guiding star,
That rudderless my lonely bark,
    Is wafted near or drifted far
With flapping sail and broken spar?
    What matters it though tempests rave,
That white with rage life's billows are?
    'Twill all be calm when in the grave.

Why should I care how goes the world,
    When not a worldling cares for me?
The showers of hate upon me hurled
    Have seared my heart to sympathy,
Though bliss or woe around I see,
    To me they both appeal in vain;
My heart. chilled into apathy,
    May never smile or weep again.

But it is useless to complain,
    Despite the darkness, I must on,
Until shall end in woe and pain,

A life in pain and woe begun,
My race through life I still must run
    Though course and goal be wrapped in gloom,
And only hope when all is done,
    To find a Lethe in the tomb.

GOD ALWAYS HELPS THE POOR.

TELL me not that fame and power,
    Are not for those who're humbly born ;
That only by the favored few,
    The laurels of success are worn,
Say not that to the rich and great
    Alone, are Fortune's breezes given,
And that the poor, though wise and good,
    Can ne'er receive the smile of Heaven ;
God doth not regulate his love
    By hoarded piles of glittering store,

And where the heart and mind are right,
  He loves to aid the suffering poor.

It is a *holy heart desire,*
  That Heaven doth delight to bless ;
And 'tis a well-directed MIND,
  That earns the honors of success,
And where the heart and mind are stirred,
  With noble thoughts, and high desires,
That soul shall sure attain its end,
  Though it in victory's arms expires.

Why hath God planted in my breast,
  One independent wish or thought,
If in his soul He deemed it best
  Those wishes all should come to naught ?
Would He torment a struggling soul
  With high ambition's lofty pride,—
With hopes which ere that soul was formed,
  He knew ne'er could be gratified ?
No, though our earthly lot is cast,
  In humble cots, or halls of pride,
No holy wish e'er filled or hearts,
  That may not yet be gratified.

If I could believe that in my heart,
   Ambition's longings were in vain,
I'd snap the thread of life apart,
   And sink at once to death's domain,
But while I believe that God is just,
   The star of hope still brightly burns,
And shall until success is won,
   And hope to full fruition turns.

TO ELLA.

WHEN Fate declared our lives must part,
 I meekly met its stern decree,
And deemed that time would in my heart,
 Soon quench each cherished thought of thee.

I hoped that care my heart would steel,
 I hoped that toil might Lethe prove,
That time the aching wounds would heal
 Caused by the pangs of hopeless love.

Ah me ! how vain I've found that hope—
 How vain the hope must e'er be found,
That aught on earth can ever cope
 With Passion's never-healing wound.

The fiercest hate may cease to burn;
   The brightest hopes may fade and fly;
And warmest friendships oft may turn
   Into a heartless apathy.

But when true love once thrills the breast,
   Through time and change it still glows on,
And ne'er again knows peace or rest
   Until Affection's goal is won.

The passing years that o'er it glide,
   May strive, perchance, the heart to steel,
But O, how vain! time can but hide,
   The wounds she vainly seeks to hear.

The wintry northwind's chilling breath,
   Congeals the surface of the river,
But the bright stream that flows beneath,
   Must still flow on, as bright as ever.

So, with the wounds that Passion makes,
   Time's wintry hand the scar may cover,
But when the heart beneath them breaks,
   It broken must remain forever.

So, though my heart seems dead and cold,
   And hope has fled before despair,
The love that warmed my heart of old,
   Still burns as bright as ever there.

Though months and years of toil and care,
   Have glided by since last we met,
Yet still (as Hope shines o'er despair),
   Thy face shines through my memory yet.

Still fly my thoughts on fancy's wings,
   Back to the hour when thou wert mine ;
Still memory 'round those moments clings,
   Like Faith around its cherished shrine.

And though those hours are gone and past,
   And ne'er on earth to me'll return,
Still must thine image haunt my breast,
   Till life's thin lamp shall cease to burn.

And though my life is dark and void,
   And all that's past seems but a dream,
And all that e'er my soul enjoyed,
   But makes life's darkness darker seem.

Yet could I believe the vows thou made'st,
　　When Passion's leaves were fresh and green,
When on my breast thy head thou laid'st
　　And vowed that naught should come between.

Could I believe the vows then made,
　　Were fondly cherished still by thee,
Then howsoever dark o'erhead,
　　The clouds of fate might seem to be.

Yet, yet contented could I rest,
　　Through darkest hours of gloom and ill,
And feel myself supremely blest,
　　In knowing thou wert faithful still.

TO A FRIEND.

HOW rarely, O! how rarely! as we roam
  Through life's dark, dreary desert do we meet
With places where the flowers of friendship bloom,
Untainted by the poison of deceit!
How rarely is the smile which doth us greet,
More than a mask to hide a traitor's schemes!
How oft are we allured by phrases sweet,
Into misfortune's ways, until it seems
True friendship doth exist but in some poet's dreams.

O then how pleasant 'tis to find a spot
Where pure, devoted friendship can be found,
Where the sweet smile, or friendly grasp is not
A snare to lure us on to treacherous ground!
How blest is he who in life's lonely round,
Can feel that one true friend at least, will be
With him, in bonds of firmest friendship bound;
How near to heaven on earth indeed, is he
Who in this treacherous world, can find one friend
    like thee!

TO A LADY.

WHEN life's dark desert journeying o'er,
   Some field of daisies glads the eye,
So oft we've seen the same before,
   We scarcely glance while passing by,
But when some blushing rose we 'spy,
   Smiling its thanks to Beauty's giver,
O then we longer gaze, and sigh,
   Because we cannot gaze forever.

This, this is why amid the fair,
   And tempting forms that 'round I see,
My wandering glance from them must e'er
   Return to fix itself on thee,
And sure my boldness thou'lt forgive.—
   Forgive the rudeness of my glance,
Since though I might for ages live,
   Such charms I'd never meet but once

THOUGHTS SUGGESTED BY CHILD HAROLD.

I.

BYRON! thou of such dazzling powers possessed !
  Thou greatest master of the "Art Divine,"
Thou whom, though cursed by man, the Muses blessed
  With supernatural genius ! what a mine
  Of wealth, are thee, thy pages ! Every line
Gleams with some blushing beauty of the mind,
  Till like a galaxy, the pages shine,
O, where in poesy's kingdom shall we find
One who has left so grand a monument behind ?

II.

Men call thee atheistical, and sneer
  At thy dark musings, but — were they not true ?
What *is* man but a helpless waif, thrown here,

And there, by Fortune's fickle breezes?   Do
  Not all things in us, and about us, show
That men are but as are the motes that play
  In every sunbeam where a breath may blow?
Do we not float all heedless, as do they?
And like them sink to earth, when life's breath dies away?

III.

Men long have dreamed of immortality,
  Wherein *something*, which they call the soul,
Shall dwell for aye in bliss or misery,
  But no man yet hath seen that distant goal;
  Though the flood of time doth onward roll,
Yet as a boundless sea spread out before,
  Of which no man may ever see the whole,
Though ever its wide billows hurrying o'er,—
Thus doth the future yawn, and shall forevermore!

IV.

Man is but dust, and shall to dust return,
  To rise in other forms, but still no more,
Than common dust; though he may incense burn,
  To unknown beings; and bow down before
  Their shrines to worship, and in fancy soar
To brain-born lands of bliss beyond the skies,
  Still he no higher gets, but rather lower;

Though he in different forms from earth may rise,
In each succeeding form the greater meanness lies.

V.

Existence is at best a mystery ;
   Awhile we flourish, then is death decay,
And one score words may write our history ;—
    " Their courses they have run, and passed away,
    And naught remaineth but their lifeless clay ! "
This is the whole, and yet we dream of lands,
   Of bliss or woe, in endless night or day,
Where souls shall live, in homes not made with hands—
Things no man ever sees, or even understands !

VI.

Who understands man's dreams of hell or heaven ?
   Who knoweth what they are, or where they be ?
What are those sins he fain would have forgiven ?
   What is that soul which pays their penalty ?
   If they are anything, 'tis mystery
Beyond our comprehension, and we are
   Not called to believe that for which we can see
No evidence, and why then should we care
If such exist at all ? or what they are, or where ?

VII.

The soul is but the mind, no more, no less ;
   Sin is the breaking of mankind's decrees ;
Heaven is each one's idea of happiness ;
    And Hell 's the essence of all miseries,
    Where each and every one in fancy sees
His foes, the fruit of all their failings, reap ;
   But which each locates wheresoe'er he please ;
Death is a dreamless, though eternal sleep,
Or at worst, from light to darkness, but a leap.

VIII.

Death is, we know, a stern reality,
   But all the rest are fictions, and we know,
That 'tis the nature of mortality,
    To cling to fancies, and of facts let go ;
    In sooth, methinks sometimes 'tis better so,
For some on hope can live, and happy be,
   Though others on such food would only grow
To feel more keen their present misery,
Since in the great BEYOND, no ray of light they see !

TO --—.

———

WHEN, o'er the western skies the hues of even,
　　Have spread their tints of purple and of gold ;
When, through the azure of the twilight heaven,
The evening stars their twinkling wealth unfold ;
When the bright Bow of Promise we behold
Spanning with beauty, earth from shore to shore ;
When any form of Beauty's heavenly mould,
　Shines brightly our be-darkened souls before,
What can we do but bow, and fervently adore ?

But through bright Nature's spreading realms, though
　　　there
May many a form of light and beauty shine ;
Though in the earth, the sky, the sea, the air,
May sparkle many a gem from Beauty's mine,

Yet vain I seek for beauty like to thine ;
Though 'mong the charms which our existence bless,
May some be found which almost seem divine,
In thee alone would Nature fain express
In Beauty's matchless lines, Perfection's loveliness.

Not the bright stars that shine o'er us at even ;
Not the bright sunset, with its varying dyes;
Not the bright rainbow, spanning earth and heaven ;
Nor all the forms of beauty 'neath the skies,
Can match the beauty of thy matchless eyes !
As full and soft as evening stars they roll,
Yet more than starlight in their brightness lies,
So dark, so deep, so wildly beautiful,
So filled with inward light, like mirrors of the soul.

Well hath the poet sung, such eyes are given
To nurse our hopes of immortality,
To show that e'en on earth exists a heaven
Of Beauty, Truth, and inward purity !
O ! who can believe, when gazing upon thee,
That youth can ever fade, or beauty die ?
To bowers elysian it from earth may flee,
But who can gaze upon that melting eye,
And doubt 'twas born to shine in brighter worlds on high.

And when in life my weary soul despairs,
And all around can naught but darkness see,
Then may my every thought, my hopes, my prayers,
Be led to heaven by gazing upon thee !
Nay ! where thou art shall seem like heaven to me !
And though Hope's star may o'er me cease to shine,
Thy memory still my guiding star shall be,
Still shall this longing heart hail thee divine,
And ask no dearer heaven than those sweet eyes of thine !

TO A PHOTOGRAPH.

LAS! why did I ask to see
   The pictured face of her I loved,
And fondly believe my heart could be
   No more by its dear beauty moved?
Why did I believe, though hope was o'er,
   That passion ne'er might burn again,
And that for her I cared no more,
   Who once I loved, but loved in vain.

I might have known that hearts can never
   Grow cold, when once they've learned to love;
But still must like a wintry river,
   Glow on, though all's congealed above,
I might have known, though cold despair,
   Had chilled my heart and seared my brain,
The sight of charms so treasured there,
   Would start them into life again.

But it is done ! The wound is oped
  Afresh, which death alone can heal ;
The pang is felt which I had hoped
  My heart again might never feel,
That pang, which I can ne'er forget,
  So life-like drawn by Summer's beam ;
Has in my soul a flame re lit
  Which naught can quench but Lethe's stream.

And yet more than all else below,
  That face is to my memory dear ;
Whate'er I do, where'er I go,
  It seems forever hovering near.
Like that star which, when cast away,
  The mariner hails with such delight,
For though it proves he's gone astray,
  Its twinkling beams will guide him right.

Thus, thus, as to that lonely star,
  From life's dark flood I look to thee ;
And though from me thou'rt severed far.
  Thou still my star of hope shall be,
Thy face, by sunbeams here impressed,
  Forever close my heart shall wear,
To keep alive within my breast,
  The cherished memories lingering there.

TO LOLA.

———

YOU ask how I, who seem so gay
　　When Pleasure's cup is circling 'round,
Upon whose lip the smiles alway
　　Of seeming happiness are found,
How I who seem so light and glad,
　　As I have always seemed to you,
Can write such gloomy things and sad,
　　And dark and wild, I sometimes do?

Ah ! Lola, darling, there are hearts
　　Too stern to break, too proud to yield,
Which 'gainst misfortune's firiest darts,
　　Are, to all outward seeming steeled,
Which when Despair the soul is racking,
　　Can wreathe the lips in smiles of joy,
And when the heart seems almost breaking,
　　Can hide the pangs which would destroy.

But think not sorrows thus concealed,
    Are felt the less when curtained o'er,
The very power that keeps them veiled,
    But makes their anguish felt the more,
For Ætna burns as fiercely now,
    Down in her rock-bound cell confined,
As when in mad irruption's glow
    She blazed, the terror of mankind.

And truly, Lola, I have felt
    What adverse fate can shower on man,
In dark misfortune's caves I've dwelt,
    Since first my weary life began,
Foul Disappointment aye hath blighted
    The fondest hopes I ever cherished,
And every flower that might have lighted
    My life, has ere its blooming, perished.

True I have felt no crushing blow,
    Such as one well might perish under,
But man a deadlier pang can know
    Than that which snaps life's thread asunder,
'Tis when those minor hopes, which seem
    Like stars that gem the skies at even,—

When these are quenched in Misery's stream,
  Then death itself would seem like heaven !

This I have felt and lived to bear,
  And learned to crush the rising groan,
Save when, like breathings of Despair,
  They struggle forth when all alone,
And it is better thus to find
  A vent, than ne'er to 'scape at all,
For if they always filled my mind
  They'd turn my very soul to gall.

Then wonder not, when next you turn
  These pages filled with darksome dreams,
How they can thus with misery burn,
  When he who writes so joyous seems ;
Remember Pride can conquer woe,
  And bear the wound that knows no cure,
And hearts that break not 'neath the blow.
  Can learn in silence to endure !

LIFE.

WHEN the roses of Childhood are strewing the way,
    And life seems as bright as a mid-summer day,
Untaught by remembrance of days that are past,
We deem that such brightness forever can last.

But Time, like a river, flows ceaselessly on,
And soon all the brightness of Childhood is gone
And the flowers that we love, and the hopes that we cherish,
Like early spring blossoms, soon wither and perish.

'Neath the hot, scorching rays of the noon's blazing tide,
The well springs of fancy and feeling are dried,
And the fountain of hope which our spirits hath fed,
Like desert streams, soon withers up in its bed.

The friends which in childhood so dearly we loved,
Have flown with the years, or but traitors have proved,
And each promise of joy which our childhood held forth,
Is sered like a flower 'neath the wind of the north.

The noonday glides past, and the evening draws nigh,
And the dark clouds of grief are o'erhanging the sky,
And the life that once seemed like a flower-bed in bloom,
Grows gloomy are dark as the gates of the tomb.

And long ere the close of our life draweth near,
Naught is left us to hope, naught is left us to fear,
For the past and the present can claim but a sigh,
And we have but one wish for the future — to die.

For fell disappointment with withering blight,
Has quenched all our hopes in the darkness of night,
And the ne'er-ebbing billows of sorrow and care,
Have flooded our souls like the waves of Despair.

But one source of solace, one Lethean wave
Remains to us then ; — it is found in the grave,
And we long for the hour that shall bid us to come,
And escape from our woes in the depths of the tomb.

There, there, and there only, the soul can forget
That the sun of its morning in darkness hath set,
And there, and there only, disappointments shall cease,
And Eternity glide like an ocean of Peace.

FAREWELL.

FAREWELL, and farewell, and forever ;
    Be it mine to forgive and forget,
And be it thy destiny, never
    The step thou hast ta'en, to regret,
Farewell ! though my heart is 'most broken,
    And broken, fair false one, by thee,
Not one evil wish shall be spoken,
    Or thought for a moment, by me.

I loved with a love that was holy,
    And tender and pure as the skies ;

I loved — but my passion was folly,
  For lovers can never be wise !
I loved with a love deep and yearning ;
  I hoped with a hope bright as day ;
That hope perished soon, but the burning,
  Of passion shall linger for aye !

Farewell ! and may blessings and blisses
  Fall on thee in Heaven sent showers,
And may time flow as light as the kisses
  A butterfly drops among flowers ;
Every moment that passes thee over
  May the roses of pleasure bewreathe,
And O ! may thou never discover
  The thorns that are lurking beneath.

Farewell ! may the Heavens above thee
  Watch o'er thee, and guard thee, and guide ;
May those whom thou love, and who love thee,
  Be found ever close at thy side ;
May the pathways of pleasure and duty,
  Forever for thee intertwine,
And the smiles and the blessings of Beauty
  And Virtue, forever be thine.

Farewell, and farewell, and forever,
　　I leave thee to journey afar,
To seek for some Lethean river,
　　Whose billows can conquer despair,
And, till its dark waves I sink under,
　　My soul must live on in its pains,—
Must aimless and hopelessly wander
　　'Mid gloom that is blacker than Cain's.

Farewell once again, and forever;
　　To linger here sighing were vain,
Since over my destiny never
　　May the rainbow of hope smile again,
Farewell! wheresoe'er may be driven,
　　My bark over Destiny's sea,
I will ask but one favor of Heaven —
　　Its blessing on thine, and on thee.

THE SADDEST OF ALL.

'TIS sad to see some flower we fondly cherish,
　　Nipt by an early autumn's blighting frost ;
'Tis sad to see our fondest wishes perish,
　　Till life seems stript of all we prized the most.

'Tis sad to see a mother bending over
　　The open coffin of her first-born child :
'Tis sad to see a maiden, by her lover,
　　Wronged and deserted, till her brain runs wild.

'Tis sad to see, amid the waves of ocean.
　　A noble bark go down with all her crew ;
'Tis sad to see a friend on whose devotion,
　　You would have staked your fortune, prove untrue.

'Tis sad to see a youth, by aspiration,
  And Nature formed to lead in glory's chase,
Led by false friends, and reckless dissipation,
  Down the steep road to ruin and disgrace.

'Tis sad to see a lovely maid, death-smitten,
  Sink like a snow-cloud which the sunshine melts ;
But sadder far it is to get the " mitten,"
  And see your girl go home with some one else !

UNCHANGING.

———

IT is not true as the words of sages
  Saith, that the world is changing aye,
The world was the same in the long gone ages,
  As it will be to-morrow, and is to-day.

The years go on, and the world goes over,
  And men as of old, are born to sigh,

To love, and to hope ; and live to discover,
  That love is a snare, and that hope is a lie.

In all the years of the misty past
  Men have loved and have sighed in vain ;
And in all the years to come, till the last,
  Ahey must needs be taught the old lesson again.

Past, present, and future, will men be the same ;
  They will hope, and love, and regret and sigh,
And flutter 'round Beauty like moths around flame,
  Till it scorches their life, and they sink and die !

The world does not change, howe'er it seemeth,
  Only our minds have gone astray,
As the Fancy sees when a person dreameth,
  Scenes fairer than ever were seen by day.

COURTING IN THE COUNTRY.

THE church was filled to overflowing,
  The holy service said, and o'er,
And rushing pell-mell, outward going,
  Departing footsteps press the floor,
Within the vestry as they stand,
  Two youths approach two ladies bright,
And taking each his hat in hand,
  Ask, " May I see you home to-night ?"

" No, thank you," is the cold reply,
  And with blank looks they turn away ;
But soon two other maids they 'spy,
  And unto them, the same words say,
With " No, I thank you," still they're met ;
  But still they try, and try again ;
And all the answer they can get,
  Is " No," in tones of deep disdain.

Though full four times they're thus refused,
    They try once more, with faith sublime,
So many "Noes" but got them used
    To wearing "mitts" in summer time.
Though still refused they don't despair,
    But thought 'twas getting warm just then,
And rushed out into cooler air,
    Before they dared to try again.

Says Jim, " I'll tell you what we'll do
    To get a lady-love, to-night ;
There of young maidens, still are two
    Who have not given us the slight
They both were here at church this even,
    And have but a short time been gone,—
And fairer maids, the light of Heaven
    I'm certain ne'er shone down upon !

" They both the same sweet title bear,
    For both are "Idas,"—both are young—
And both possess such charms as ne'er
    Were yet by love-sick poet sung,
We'll chase them up, and offer them
    What others here have meanly slighted,

And as the night is dark, why, dem—
  Me, if they will not be delighted ! "

"Agreed ! " and on this mission bent,
  Adown the gloomy road together,
With rapid steps they gayly went,
  With hearts as buoyant as a feather,
The night was dark, but naught they feared,
  They cared not for the world beside ;
So to the forms for which they steered,
  They grew more near at every stride.

At length they, through the gloom, espy
  The forms which have their hearts in-
      flamed ;
And gazing with an artist's eye
  Upon them, Jim to Fred exclaimed :
" I for the taller one will make,
  For wondrous beauty doth adorn her ;
But come, let's haste, and overtake
  Them ere they get to Cole's Corner ! "

With quickened pace they hurried on,
  (So seek their nests the wandering doves,)

And ere the Corner-post was won,
  They both had reached their lady-loves,
And, " May I see you home to-night?"
  With beating hearts, they softly say.
And both reply, with glances bright,
  " You can *the rest, sir, of the way !* "

With arm in arm, and softened voices,
  Adown the gloomy road they passed ;
And doubtless every one rejoices,
  That they obtained a prize at last,
But what sweet things were said that night,
  Ere each had reached his love's abode,
It were a shame for me to write,
  And so I'll leave them, on the road.

THERE IS PEACE IN THE TOMB.

AS we roam through this world's dreary desert of wrong,
Many trials and sorrows around us may throng,
But whatever afflictions upon us may come,
It is pleasing to think they will cease in the tomb.

When the pathway of life is o'er-shadowed with woe,
And wrecked is each hope we have cherished below,
When keen disappointments our spirits benumb,
It is soothing to think there is peace in the tomb.

When the past is all checkered with sufferings and tears,
And never a light in the future appears ;
When the present is thickly enveloped in gloom,
We still can look on to the rest of the tomb.

When friends have deserted, and loved ones betrayed,
And fortune her forces hath 'gainst us arrayed,
When our firesides the seat of the stranger become,
O ! still there is refuge, at least in the tomb.

When there's not one kind heart in Humanity's sea,
To which, with the tale of our woes we can flee,
Our grief-laden bosoms a rest, and a home,
Can find in the chilling embrace of the tomb.

Oh! why then complain of the sorrow and strife,
That meets us for aye, in our journey through life,
When soon we shall cease through its sufferings to roam,
And rest in the sweet, dreamless sleep of the tomb.

THE "ENTIRE SANCTIFICATIONISTS."

ALAS! love of justice compels me to say,
　　That full oft from the ways of their Master they fall,
And though loudly they sing, and though warmly they pray,
　　Yet they scarce to perfection attain after all!

They think themselves saints, and almost into Heaven,
　　But a spark of old Adam burns bright in them still,
And as one grain of leaven, the whole lump will leaven,
　　So that little spark their whole bosoms doth fill.

The fruit of a tree is the test of its worth,
　　And applying this test to the Perfectly Whole,
We find that they too like the rest of the earth
　　Still carry the trade-mark of Sin in the soul.

THE CITY OF——.

A Fragment.

SOCIETY is there, (as elsewhere, I suppose,)
    Made up of saints and sinners, prudes and rakes.
Of drunkards and teetotalers,—God knows
    Why, when a city, or a world he makes,
The good, bad, and indifferent, he throws
    Promiscuously together, and then takes
The good to task if on their snowy banners,
He finds the slightest stain of evil manners.

Yet so it is ; I know not why 'tis so,
    Unless to make the bright still brighter shine,
By contrast to the darker ; or to show
    That from the mire and clay which forms the mine,
The glittering diamond may come forth, and glow
    With light so dazzling as to seem divine,
Or else, perhaps it is designed to show,
That all are evil, but none wholly so !

TOIL ON.

TOIL on ! toil on ! nor faint, my brother,
    Though hope may dimly o'er you shine ;
Though failure oft your hopes may smother,
    Some meed of glory shall be thine,
'Twere better far to strive, and die
    Unblest by all we hoped to gain,
Than coward-like, to sit and sigh,
    For crowns we dare not try obtain.

Though neither you nor I, my brother,
    May soar to Glory's summit quite,
This joy is ours, e'en though no other,
    To reach at least, some lower hight,
And this deserveth praise alone,
    For though we short of Glory fall.
Yet millions are who die unknown,
    And never dare soar at all.

THE STAR OF FAME.

— —

AS erst the ignis fatuus flame,
  Lured unsuspecting travelers far
O'er yielding quicksands, which became
  The grave of all who ventured there.

So does the gilded Star of Fame,
  Lure on Ambition's reckless slaves,
O'er fields of care, and toil, and shame,
  To find therein untimely graves!

THE TEST OF WORTH!

A Fragment.

THOUGH some good things remain to us yet,
  'Tis a mighty strange age, on the whole, you bet,
And we see strange sights, and we hear strange sounds,
And many strange jokes are agoing the rounds,
But the funniest joke of them all, I guess,
Is that virtue can dwell in a calico dress!
Why, bless your soul! do you know that as things
Are now, you must look at a woman's rings,
And measure the grandeur of her coiffure,
To find if she's morally good or pure!
The time was erst in the days of old,
When worth was worth its weight in gold,
And a cultured mind, and a spotless heart,
Were valued higher than gems of art,
E'en though adorning the pampered heir,
Of the nation's mightiest millionaire.

Now, mind and heart at a discount go,
And the test of worth is the outward show,
And the more of jewels and gold you wear,
(No matter how got), the better you are,
For 'tis never asked what a man can do,
And 'tis never asked if a maid be true,
A man may be wiser than Solomon's self,
And 'twill go for naught, if he lacks for pelf,
And a maid may be lovely, and pure and chaste,
As the fairest lily that ever was traced,
But they'll ne'er be considered the salt of the earth,
Till the earth finds out what their bank-book's worth.

A THOUGHT.

———

WHEN, plunging from some overhanging shore,
  We sink beneath the waves that roll below,
The higher up the starting-point, the lower
  Into the ocean's briny depths we go.

So, when we headlong from some moral brink,
  Plunge, and the waves of crime our souls enthrall,
The depth in vice to which our spirits sink,
  Proportions to the hight from which we fall.

IF ALL OUR HOPES AND ALL OUR FEARS.

IF all our hopes, and all our fears,
  Were for our choice, before us cast,
And only smiles, or only tears,
  Could be our doom while life should last.
'Twixt ceaseless bliss and ceaseless woe,
  ''Twere hard to tell the best, or worst,
Or, since we only one could know,
  To tell of which we'd sicken first.

Oft when our hopes are realized,
  And fortune crowns us with success,
We find the things so dearly prized,
  More prone to curse us than to bless ;
And oft 'mid darkest hours of ill,
  Some moments are supremely bright,
And woe's sensations sometimes thrill
  Our souls more sweetly than delight.

A SOUTH SEA LOVE SONG.

WHEN the moon is at its full,
  And when the stars are at their brightest,
When the breezes murmur cool,
  And when the waves are swelling lightest,
When the fairy chains of slumber
  Fall on heaven, earth and sea,
Then, my darling am I thinking,
  Thinking darling one of Thee.

When the rosy beams of morning
  Like a cheering angel come,
And the day's resplendent dawning,
  Chases night's repelling gloom,
When the flowers to life are springing,

And the birds are warbling free,
Then my darling, am I thinking,
    Thinking, darling one, of Thee.

When the gathering shades of even,
    Spread their purple o'er the skies,
And adown the western heaven
    Sinks the sunset's varying dyes,
When the twilight softly deepens
    Over isle and over sea,
Then, my darling, am I thinking,
    Thinking, darling one, of Thee.

BEAUTY.

"Oh! if such magic power there be,
This, this," he cried, "is all my prayer,
To catch the living light I see.
And fix the soul that sparkles there."

'TIS not alone the faultless form,
  And chiseled face,
The classic beauty's matchless charm,
  And witching grace ;
'Tis not in these we always seek
  Our heart's ideal,
The brightest rose may tint the cheek,
The deepest night may tinge the eyes,
The face may be like April skies,
  And yet lack still,
The gem whose brightness doth outshine the whole—
  A kindred soul.

And where this gem we find, though naught beside,
  May charm us there,

Nor gracefullness, nor symmetry, nor pride,
    Nor features fair,
Yet if there, through a spirit shines,
    Refined and pure,
We miss not Beauty's matchless lines ;
We only see the pearl we prize,
Nor rosier cheeks, nor brighter eyes,
    Can e'er allure.
Or tempt us thence, or our affections move,
    From her we love.

The sculptured marble, though of perfect mould,
    No feeling knows ;
The rose of wax, though pleasant to behold,
    Is not the rose.
And so there are some living forms,
    No soul inherit,
To light and grace their lifeless charms ;
And though their beauty we awhile admire ;
We of 'such soul-less loveliness soon tire,
    But where the spirit,
Of Beauty is, it ne'er can fail to move
    Our hearts to love.

LIFE.

———

WHAT has death that we should fear?
What has life that we should crave?
In Earth's dark and drear,
But one oasis doth appear,
Only one, and that — the grave.

Life is like a desert waste,
Pleasures like the mirage are,
Vainly by the traveler chased,
Ever sought, but ne'er embraced,
Ever near, yet ever far.

Life is like a boundless ocean,
We like voyagers sailing o'er,

Joy is like the enchanted isles.
Which the longing soul beguiles,
   Onto some death-haunted shore.

Life is like a barren heath,
   Bliss is like the *ignis* flame,
Luring on to certain death,
In the quicksands hid beneath —
   Quicksands of remorse and shame.

DESPAIR.

WHEN over life's tempestuous path,
　Hope's star is still, though dimly, shining
And through the tempest's fiercest wrath,
　The clouds still show their silver lining,
Then may we dare to struggle on,
　Though storm and darkness rage awhile,
And hope ere life is fully gone,
　To bask at length in Glory's smile.

But when Hope's star has set forever,
　And midnight's gloom the soul enshrouds,
And o'er the dark horizon never
　A rift appears among the clouds,
When over Desperation's brink
　Our lives, and hopes, and fortunes hover,
Then well the strongest soul may think
　'Twere better far, if all were over.

A SONNET.

———

IF any man is brave enough to live,
  And bear unflinchingly the ceaseless woes
Which Fate reserves for man ; if he can strive
    With fears, false friends, false hopes, and treach-
        erous foes,
'Til his life's day shall nearly reach its close,
And then look backward with exultant eye,
And find no spot upon his past career,
Where he hath added to another's woes,
Or in another's eye hath caused a tear,
And then without one vain regret or fear,
Can calm and cheerful lay him down to die,
That man is a true hero, though his lot
Be cast among the lowly, and his name,
Unblazoned on the dazzling scroll of Fame,

Be in one year, or month, or day, forgot,
For 'tis not death, but life, that tries the soul,
And if a man has strength to bear,
Nor in impatience early, seek the goal,
But to the end can bravely persevere,
He need not tremble for the final hour,
He hath already felt all death can give,
And death for them has lost its stinging power,
Who uncomplainingly have learned to live.

TRANSIENT.

EVERYTHING that's bright and fair,
　　Everything we seek or prize,
Like the purple hues of even,
Like the arching bow of heaven,
Like a flower by tempests rive,n
　　Smiles, and fades and dies.

One by one our pleasures fade,
　　One by one our joys are past,
Soon of all that lured us on,
Every shining flower is gone,
Only treacherous Hope alone,
　　Lingers to the last.

CHRISTMAS.

O scatter the roses of pleasure around,
  For but once in our lives do they blossom so brightly,
And think not of the thorns that are lurking to wound
  The fingers that clasp them too rudely and tightly.

Let us quaff of the goblet of bliss in full measure,
  When Infancy's roses, Life's pathway are strewing,
And forget for a moment that mornings of pleasure
  May end in dark noondays of sorrow and ruin.

TOM PAINE.*

———

" Unanswered and, unmatched he died,
The free alone revere his name."
—CLINT PARKHURST.

'TWAS 'mid the gloom of Slavery's night,
  When Freedom seemed, or dead, or dreaming,
And not one ray of Truth or Right,
  Was o'er the world's horizon gleaming,
'Twas then the immortal Paine uprose,
  As rose the gods in ancient story,

---

* Among all the heroes of our Revolution, few, if any, deserved better or have received worse treatment, than Tom Paine. At the close of the Revolutionary War he was one of the most popular men in America. He was the bosom friend of Washington, Jefferson, and the other respected leaders of the country. His services in the cause had been second to none. His COMMON SENSE first showed the people their right to be free, and his CRISIS, which was ordered by Washington to be read before each regiment of the army, was the star of hope which cheered the patriots in their weary struggle. Had he died then, his name would now be one of the brightest in our history. But he saw that the mass of mankind were as much slaves to Ignorance, Bigotry, and Prejudice, as they had ever been to the British Lion. To free them from this bondage he wrote the AGE OF REASON, and from that moment his reputation was doomed. At once were forgotten all his

And fired the beacon which still glows,
   The freeman's hope, and patriot's glory.

'Twas not for him to bend the knee,
   Before Injustice crowned and thronely—
The ordained champion of the free,
   He lived and fought for freedom only,
And fired with holy love for men,
   For truth, for freedom, and for reason,
He boldly bore their banners, when
   To love was crime, to praise was treason,

No coward fear could turn aside,
   Or swerve him from the path of duty,
'Til man, with every bond untied,

---

eminent talents, his public and private virtues, and his disinterested labors in the cause of freedom and humanity. All these were swept away in the whirlwind of spite which greeted the appearance of the "Infidel's Text Book." Thenceforth there was no epithet too bitter, no slander too foul, no meanness too contemptible, for the followers of Him who prayed for his murderers, to pour on the head of the once honored patriot. The ingratitude of Republics has long been a proverb, and the treatment of Thomas Paine is only another illustration of its truth. Despite the material grandeur and prosperity of this Nation, there are dark and disgraceful stains upon our escutcheon that an immortality of glory will scarcely efface, and among the blackest of them all will yet be considered our shameful treatment of the "Author hero of the Revolution."

Should stand erect in Nature's beauty,
And till on Glory's lofty hight,
　Where gathered stand earth's brightest sages,
His name should shine a beacon light,
　Of truth and hope to future ages.

And there to-day he stands enshrined,
　'Mid brightest flowers of Glory's wreathing,
Adored by each and every mind,
　Worthy the gifts of his bequeathing.
And while the hosts of Wrong remain,
　And priests and tyrants still shall lead 'em,
The name and works of Thomas Paine
　Shall be the battle cry of Freedom.

I THINK OF THEE.

A Parody.

"I think of thee, I think of thee."
—G. D. Prentice.

WHEN in the morn the rooster crows,
    And from my nightly couch I rise,
And say my prayers, and don my clothes,
    And brush the cobwebs from my eyes,
When underneath my curled mustache,
    (Which thou hast often smiled to see),
I stow my morning's dish of hash,
    I think of thee, I think of thee.

I think of thee when evening calls
    The bat and hoot-owl from their lair,

And the musquito's music falls
　　Upon the ague-laden air,
And when their never ceasing hum
　　Hath driven slumber far from me,
Till life seems like the life to come —
　　I think of thee, I think of thee.

WOMAN.

"Whose name is as blessing to speak."
　　　　　　　—SWINBURNE.

THE sun of Life's morning, the star of Life's even,
　The rainbow of Hope in Life's storm-darkened heaven,
Where'er in the darkness of Life's gloomy round
Heaven's light is most needed, there Woman is found.

The fountain that springs in Earth's desert of woe,
The flower that blooms brightest where'er we may go,

The pole-star of guidance o'er Life's stormy tide,
Ever Woman, blest woman is close by our side.

To solace our sorrow, to lighten our care,
To guide us in trouble, to soothe in despair,
To bless with a smile or to cheer with a kiss —
O ! what blessing hath heaven more precious than this?

Like the ivy that twines around storm-beaten towers,
Woman's love is strongest in the stormiest hours,
And though floods of disaster her loved ones o'ertake,
She will suffer and perish, but never forsake.

EVOLUTION.

———

IF those who sneer at Darwin's plan,
  About the true " Descent of Man,"
Would work the vexing problem out,
And prove its truth beyond a doubt,
Methinks they only need to pass
Before a first-rate looking-glass !

FREE SALVATION.

"They tell us that Salvation 's free! Free! It takes a California
gold mine every year to pay expenses.—COMMON SENSE.

"SALVATION 's free," the preacher cries,
  "Free as the glorious light of day.
But if the precious gift you prize,
  Just pass your mites this way.

" Come without money, without price,
  The rich, the poor, the great, the small,
But don't forget the widow's mites!—
  'Tis grand to give your all!

A WORD AT PARTING.

—

O, little book, upon thy dangerous way ;
　To make thee worthy I have done my best,
And if thou fail'st to live thy "little day,"
　The fault with thee, and thee alone, must rest,
My hopes are for thy good ; I warmly pray
　That the dull world will recognize thy worth,
And if at last thou thy expenses pay,
Despite what envious critics choose to say,
　Then shall I not regret thy having birth.